EYE

OF
THE

TIGER

A Nick Ryan Mystery Thriller
by

Bryan Mooney

Novels by Bryan Mooney

Christmas in Vermont—*A Very White Christmas*
A Box of Chocolates
Love Letters
A Second Chance

- Mystery Thrillers -
Eye of the Tiger—*A Nick Ryan Mystery Thriller*
The POTUS Papers—*A Nick Ryan Mystery Thriller*
INDIE—*A Female Vigilante*

Books are available wherever fine books are sold.

Catawampus
1. Out of alignment, crooked, cattycorner
2. Fierce, destructive; a *fierce imaginary animal, a bogeyman*

Eye of the Tiger

A Nick Ryan Mystery Thriller
by
Bryan Mooney

Nick Ryan, a former top investigator for the FBI, is haunted by the memory of his dead wife and is struggling to move on, when a chilling message from his former partner sends him on a hunt for a killer. He soon discovers that billions of government dollars have vanished, and the journalist on the trail has gone missing.

When a beautiful woman lands on his doorstep with a mystery all her own his search soon descends into a maelstrom of corruption and terror. Nick's search leads him to wonder if a single terrorist could be behind it all. He must find an answer before more people die. Nick Ryan is running out of time. He needs to find the key to—The Eye of the Tiger.

Chapter One

February 2014

N*ick Ryan sat in the bedroom of his beach house, his eyes transfixed on his ancient answering machine. The light was no longer blinking, and his longtime friend and former partner Frank Delgado was no longer alive. His hand was shaking as he raised the drink to his lips. The bourbon was harsh as it made its way down his throat. He pressed the replay button on his answering machine and heard his old friend's familiar voice.*

"Hey Nicky, Del here. I just finished an assignment in Baghdad a few days ago with the Bureau, and now I'm on the move. I've been trackin' money, I mean a lot of money, a whole shitload, but I think they're onto me. Need to get to a safe house quick before they get me. Tried to call Washington to brief them but no luck. I wanted you to know what was going on here just in case something happens to me and...wait I'm at the safe house now." He heard Frank knock on a door and a muffled voice in the background ask, *"Come in. Who you talkin' to?"*

He heard Frank respond, *"It's okay, it's Nick Ryan back in the states. He's cool."*

"Anybody follow you?" The other voice asked in a nervous tone.

"No, nobody." Then Frank's voice became clearer as he continued dictating his message to the machine and whispered, *"Nick, I need you to do something for me. I think we have a—"* Suddenly the unmistakable sound of a bullet stopped his words in midsentence, as Nick heard the heavy thump of his former partner's body fall to the ground and his cell phone crash beside him.

There was a muted noise, then Nick heard a voice say something he would never forget, "Be careful, Mr. Ryan," and then the phone went dead.

Nick Ryan was as hardened an FBI agent as there was and he was the best they had in the field. He took another large swallow of whiskey from his half-empty glass and reached for the button to play the message once again.

He had called Delgado's cell phone but got a busy signal. Ryan immediately called his contacts at the Bureau and the local station chief. He still had plenty of friends and contacts in the FBI and other local agencies; he would find out what had happened to his former partner. Nobody knew anything. His dad said it was probably just a bad connection but his gut instinct said it was something more. He could not shake the cold feeling that ran down his spine.

Nick finished his drink and set the empty glass down on the table, still reeling from the message he just heard. *Maybe he was mistaken? Maybe his dad was right. Maybe it was static? Maybe Del just got cut off and the phone went dead? Yeah, maybe that was it?*

Outside, everything in life still appeared normal, like nothing had happened. Ocean waves continued to crash on the shore not far from his small beach cottage, while a formation of pelicans quietly soared by overhead making their way north in search of food. Kite surfers were already far out into the waves, bouncing high and floating into the sky before crashing into the waves below.

Ryan sat on the bed, his eyes frozen on the answering machine. He tried again to call Del's cell phone again and heard the following message:

THE NUMBER YOU HAVE CALLED IS NO LONGER IN SERVICE.

Two weeks later the badly decomposed body of FBI agent Frank Delgado was found floating in the Caribbean Sea, dead, with a bullet to the head. Nick Ryan knew he should have followed his instincts.

• • •

June 2014

Nick had been spent weeks anticipating a long awaited fishing trip to the Florida Keys with some old cop friends and had spent the entire morning in the garage packing up his Jeep for the excursion. He had packed all his fishing gear, his old t-shirts, cut-offs, jeans, deck shoes, and of course his bottle opener, along with his "lucky" fishing cap.

Nick always was an old-fashioned kind of guy, preferring notepads to tablets, letters to texting, and answering machines to voice mail, but the laptop was one of his few concessions to modern technology. That was the only way he could keep in touch with friends like Tony. But hell, even his dad had a computer that he used for online dating. His father was always trying to drag Nick into the twenty-first century. Maybe next year.

He shook his head. *Can a damn computer make the sweet sounds that come from a saxophone? Or the soulful sounds of a bass fiddle?* He doubted it as he listened to the mellow refrains of his John Coltrane album playing on his refurbished record player. He reread the email message before clicking the send button speeding it on its way:

Tony—
I understand work comes first, but I'd still really like to have you come to the Keys next month for a week of fishing and some card playing with some guys I know. They're all good guys, some cops, some former agency friends, and a couple still with the bureau. It's a good time. You need to get time away. Trust me—I know what I'm talking about.
Best Regards,
Nick

P.S. I have to make a decision about coming off my leave and would love to talk to you about it.
Let me know. — N

He closed the laptop and grabbed his cell phone, another gift from his dad. "You can check email, do GPS, listen to music and even call me once in a while," he father had told him. He ran his hand through his short-cropped curly blond hair, trying to shake the sand from his early morning swim. It was another hot day in south Florida. Time for a quick shower then hit the road. Then, he glanced at his watch. If he didn't hurry he was going to be late. But for some unknown reason a cold shiver of terror ran through his body. Again.

Chapter Two

✑

THIRTEEN YEARS EARLIER

September 2001

It was a clear autumn day, the kids were back in school, the leaves were falling, and America was cooling off after a long hot summer. On September 10th, 2001, Donald Rumsfeld, the United States Secretary of Defense, strode into the first-floor Pentagon press briefing room. He was about to give an extraordinary press conference regarding waste and missing funds from the Department of Defense.

Rumsfeld took to the stage, gripped the side of the wooden podium, and said, "Ladies and gentlemen, thank you for coming. Let me get right to it," he began in his usual forthright style. "According to official government estimates we cannot track some $2.3 trillion dollars in transactions here in Department of Defense," he began. "We have an enemy, not terrorists … no, our adversaries are closer to home. It is the Pentagon bureaucracy. According to a report by the Inspector General, the Pentagon cannot account for 25 percent of what it spends. I will bring all of the investigative efforts of my office to bear on this problem to find out what has happened to our taxpayer dollars."

Secretary of Defense Donald Rumsfeld had declared war. Not on foreign terrorists, but on the Pentagon's financial accounting systems, which were decades old. "We will get to the bottom of this and find out where all of that money went!" he promised the assembled crowd of reporters on hand to listen to his unprecedented news conference.

The next day, on September 11th, 2001 at 8:46 A.M., nineteen Saudi Jihadi terrorists began an American nightmare. They hijacked four civilian aircraft and crashed them into buildings and fields, killing thousands of innocent American citizens. War was declared that day. The terrorists had brought terror to America itself. The long struggle had begun.

Americans came together as never before; as a family to heal their wounds, bury their dead, grieve their losses, and turn their focus to a common enemy. Their new adversary was the extremists who threatened their country and their way of life. Forgotten was the missing $2.3 trillion dollars the defense secretary cited the day before. The missing money was no longer important to a nation in mourning.

Chapter Three

March 2003

The war room filled quickly for the presidential briefing on the upcoming attack. It was a somber meeting even though everyone agreed it was going to be a tremendous success. Four-star general Richard Alexander said, "Thank you Mr. President. We appreciate your time, and I can assure you the assault on Iraq will go off exactly as planned. Saddam Hussein will never know what hit him as we light up the sky and destroy everything he holds dear. We have teams ready to go into Iraq and put out the oil-well fires if he carries out his threat to set them afire."

"Good, very good, general. However, always remember one thing—that this is the son-of-a-bitch who years ago in Kuwait tried to assassinate my father with a car bomb, and we all know he was also behind the September 11ᵗʰ attack, in one way or another. Now it's payback time." Even though it was over ten years since the assassination attempt on his father, he never forgot.

The president turned and said to the remaining men left behind, "So gentlemen, if there is nothing else we need to go over, I have a football game on television that I would like to watch. I got twenty bucks on Texas," he quipped, tossing a football to his chief-of-staff and longtime aide, former Texas Senator Michael Trost. It was Saturday, and the president dismissed everyone.

The president and his chief of staff left the room, followed by the Secret Service and one lone attendee, Ashton Jenkins, the newest liaison to the White House, a twenty-something staffer, said, "Excuse me, Mr. President, if I could have just five minutes of your time, sir?" He stood in the rear of the room, the only one dressed in a suit and tie.

"What is it, Jenkins? Don't tell me it's that money thing again?"

"I am afraid it is, Mr. President, at least that's part of it, sir."

"Well, come on, follow me. We have exactly four minutes until kickoff, and then I'm kicking you out. Got it, son? Talk to me while we walk."

The young man, just three years out of law school, rushed to keep up with the long strides of the tall president. Ashton Jenkins's official title was White House Deputy Assistant Liaison to the State Department, but the president had hired him only as a favor to the young man's mother. Jenkins's mother and the First Lady played bridge together every Friday afternoon with the White House Bridge Club. The president tolerated Jenkins on most things because he was not afraid to speak up, but on this issue he would listen and then dismiss him. He was not about to change his mind about bombing Iraq.

"Mr. President, I urge you to reconsider this bombing strategy on Saddam Hussein."

"Yesss…," he answered the young man very slowly. He stopped walking then turned the full wrath of the presidency on this twenty-eight-year old, "Son, you don't know what the hell you're talking about. This man is going to pay and pay big. That S.O.B. tried to murder my dad in Kuwait. Do you hear me, son? He tried to blow him up with some Goddamn car bomb. He's going to pay for that." The Secret Service agents following them paused at a discreet distance waiting for Potus to continue his journey towards the media room. They remained vigilant, as always.

"Yes sir, Mr. President. I merely wanted to point out that Saddam Hussein is a *Sunni*… and is a member of the minority in Iraq. Neighboring Iran would like nothing better than to have you push him out of power and let the majority *Shiites*, like them, take over and create another Islamic state. Mr. President, I don't think that is in our nation's best interest, sir."

"Don't you think that we have given that the most careful consideration? We studied the implications very carefully for months, and the time for study is over. It's now time to act. What do you take us for, Mr. Jenkins? Fools?"

"No, Mr. President, of course not, sir. I only felt it was my duty to pass on some information…. That's all, sir."

"Well then, get on with it, Jenkins. Didn't they teach you anything at Harvard?

"Yale, sir. I'm a Yalie, just like you, sir."

"Whatever. What else?"

They turned down an outdoor hallway and entered a large conference room with multiple big-screen TVs and huge leather lounge chairs lined up in front of the televisions. The TV was showing the college pregame warm-up.

"The other thing, Mr. President, is that we are planning to bomb this third-world country to hell. They deserve it, and the man at the top needs to go. I understand that, but after we're done, all of their government agencies will be gone, overnight. We are planning to bomb, not only their army and air force but also their electrical power grids, their telephone systems, their water supplies, their banks, their supermarkets, their schools, their military bases, their police stations, their bridges, their…"

"I get the picture, what's your point?"

Jenkins stood in front of the big man's chair, blocking his view of the game. "My point is, sir, what's next? Our boys will be there on the ground doing mop-up operations. But what about the general population? Who's going to protect them, feed them, house them, and provide them food and water? How do they get to work? Who's going to stop the looters, and what about retributions with the police gone? Unfortunately, our boys will have to step in, sir, and be put in harm's way, sir. But we will also have to hire some of the Iraqis as police officers; otherwise our guys over there in uniform are sitting ducks…sir." He paused, seeing that he now had the president's full attention.

The president looked up and said in a tone of resignation, "Go on, Jenkins." He was really beginning to dislike this young staffer.

"Well sir, how do we pay them? They have no banks, no currency, no banking system, nothing sir. Their money is now worthless. We will have destroyed all their support systems."

"Can't we just give them some damn credit cards?" he asked in amazement and disgust as he looked at the young upstart and his chief of staff who joined them.

"What are they going to do with them, sir? They have no banks. No banking system. No oil revenue to pay for anything. We'll have to give them cash and not worthless Iraqi dinar, American greenbacks and tons of it. Our government will need to help restart the government and restore their basic services. Help them rebuild. They'll have nothing, sir."

"Are you trying to spoil my ballgame, young man?"

"No sir, Mr. President. But I feel it is my job to mention these things to you, that's all, sir." There, he thought, *I've said my piece and it's time to leave.* "Good day Mr. President." He started to leave to let the president and his chief of staff discuss the growing problem.

"Hold on, Jenkins, not so fast. You started this, and now you're going stay and help us figure a way out of this mess. Grab a beer, and have a seat. How much money are we talking about anyway?"

"Billions sir. It's a big country to run and pay to keep running even for such a short time."

"Hell, I can't go to Congress and ask them if they got a spare two billion dollars lying around that they aren't using, now can I? How the hell are they going to approve this? They don't want to spend money on anything, goddamn it. You see what I'm talking about? I know there's a problem in paying for this, but shit I want it done and so do the American people. Everybody on my staff has raised this question, but I'm not going to let this stop me. We'll figure out a way to come up with a billion bucks somehow."

"Twelve, sir."

"Twelve what? Twelve billion? Twelve billion dollars? Are you nuts?"

Jenkins nodded his head in agreement. "Twelve billion dollars, sir."

"Christ sakes. Well, we'll just have to use Saddam's piggy bank and his oil revenue to pay for this mess, now won't we?" he chuckled with a large grin.

"It won't be enough, Mr. President," interjected his chief of staff. "His rigs won't be operational and pumping oil for at least a year. He'll blow all the wells. Satellite surveillance shows he's already rigged all of the major wells with explosives, over eight hundred in all, sir."

"Damn. When will our dinar program be operational, Mike?" he asked, referring to the plan to print trillions of Iraqi dinars and flood the country with them.

"Mr. President, we are printing them as we speak, but we'll need a fleet of ships to supplement the nearly thirty 747 jumbo jets we are going to use. But it will take a while, sir. Each dinar is only worth about a penny in U.S. currency, sir. So it's a lot of money to transport."

"How long?"

"Months."

"Damn! Well, Jenkins what's next? Everybody keeps saying the same thing over and over again with no goddamn resolution," he asked turning back to the young upstart. "Where do you propose we get twelve billion in cash? Huh?" he raised a beer bottle in salute as the game started.

All three men were lost in thought when a few minutes later the young Yale law graduate stood and said, "That's it, Mr. President, we get it from Hussein's own piggybank! We use his own money. Years ago when the sanctions against Iraq were tightened, we set up an oil-for-food program. He put all of his oil revenue into this escrow account, and we advanced his country and his government money to buy food and medical supplies. At last count it has a balance of over twenty billion dollars in it at."

Trost chimed in, "And Mr. President when we froze all of his assets in U.S. banks there must be at least another two to four billion dollars sitting in our vaults! We'll just send them back their own money, and it takes us off the hook."

Trost took another sip of his beer, now ignoring the game on TV as he continued the planning process, "We set up a provisional authority over there to oversee the cash and the reconstruction, then ship the money from here to Iraq and distribute it out to the new ministries and whatever banks we can find. We ship them a bunch of old tens and twenties, you know, walking-around money. We fund their government and their operations with their own cash. Beautiful, I love it."

The president slapped his leg in delight, picking up where his top aide had left off, "That's it. When the dust settles and the bombing is over we petition the U.N. and Congress to release that money for humanitarian purposes and we use that to pay for all of this stuff. Voila! Problem solved. Perfect."

"Well, sir, that will work for the everyday Iraqi on the street," Jenkins whispered, "but when we have to rebuild hospitals, electrical systems, and everything else that's been destroyed it would take forever to count out millions of dollars in tens and twenties when they are loading and unloading them from the planes." He stopped for a second before continuing. "Or we can use hundred-dollar bills." The young assistant beamed at helping find part of the solution.

"Right, Jenkins. Get on it first thing tomorrow. You run with it. You're the point man. Set up some provisional authority in Iraq when the dust settles and find an Iraqi liaison in Baghdad at the finance ministry and you're in business. If you need any help, call Mike here, OK? And if there is nothing else I would like to watch my ballgame. Good night, son, good work."

The president was pleased that he had solved two problems: one, how to pay for the war and whatever reconstruction there would be, and two, how to graciously get young Ashton Jenkins out of his hair. He smiled at himself watching his young Yalie assistant leave the room. *That will teach him to open his mouth.*

Jenkins strolled out of his meeting with the president walking on air until the realization of the huge task ahead of him fully sunk in. Now he only had to arrange to have the Federal Reserve give him billions of dollars in cash over the coming years to distribute to millions of people, in the middle of the Iraqi war zone. *Piece of cake* he thought. *Time to go home and get drunk. Next time, I'll just send a memo.*

Chapter Four

Ahmed Koshari had grown up in a decidedly upper-class family, in an area outside of Baghdad. The three-story house was large by Iraqi standards with a walled entrance and a private garden to keep the nearby sounds of the street from penetrating his family's paradise. Ahmed loved the smell of the fresh lemon flowers in the springtime. He knew it signaled the summer when school was out, so he could fish and hunt with his classmates.

His mother would entertain him and his father after the servants cleared the table and left the house for the evening. She played such beautiful music on the piano; she could have been a professional musician if that had been allowed under the regime. She gave the piano a voice, a crying voice that touched the very soul of her young son Ahmed. How he worshipped her.

His father, who years earlier lost a leg in the great Iraq war, was an internationally renowned *Sunni* religious scholar, and while not political by nature, his father followed the party line to obtain the best education for his son. His brilliant son graduated from Baghdad University and then enrolled in the finest universities abroad, first Eton then Harvard.

The dark-haired young man, with the flashing eyes, a ready smile, and hot temper was quite intense, but he had no desire to follow his father into the area of religious studies. He had a head for math and was more comfortable understanding the Iraqi economy and understanding the financial system that drove the Middle East. He learned early on that the universal secret was…oil. The world was a slave to their oil. He understood what moved the oil markets on a daily basis, and he observed the pressure points which made them so volatile. He learned well.

Ahmed was hired by the Dubai International Trading Bank (DITB) once he graduated from Harvard, but he soon became disillusioned by their quiet lifestyle and lack of imagination in their oil trades. He watched, listened, and learned.

"Your time will come," his father always told him, "You just need patience."

"That is one trait I have very little use for," he always responded.

The turning point in his life came in 1999 when his kind and gentle mother, whom he adored, was taken from their home and hung upside down in the town square by Shiite terrorists after they slit her throat for playing her piano on a holy day. Ahmed vowed he would seek his revenge on those even if it took him his whole life. The incident made him hard, cold, and calculating. His world made him cruel. He soon learned patience.

It was common for Middle Eastern governments, unable or unwilling to go to war with their enemies, to finance armies of terrorists to do their bidding and thus prolong the ongoing slaughter. They financed the terrorists with their oil money, earned from oil sales to the rest of the world desperate to maintain their standard of living with foreign oil.

On the morning of September 11th, 2001, Ahmed traveled to New York City for a business meeting when the terrorists attacked the World Trade Center and annihilated thousands of innocent victims. They called it a jihad; he called it a massacre. He was detained three times while leaving the city, questioned and released. He fled to Canada where he called his father.

"Father, the Americans are in shock, but when they come to their senses and bury their dead, they will come to find those responsible. What is on the minds of these religious zealots? They are killing everyone. Now they have awakened the Americans."

"In the world of the blind, my son," he told him, "the one-eyed man is king. The Jihadists tactics have a place, but their ideology is quite suspect. Now look at what they have done. They build nothing; they simply destroy. They have only hate in their hearts. They misinterpret the holy words. They are fools. But learn from them, my son, because they are powerful in their mission. Do not underestimate them. As long as our governments have the oil money to finance their proxy wars, the slaughter will continue. But pray that the Americans never fully develop their own natural resources. They would then have the upper hand. I tasted oil once and while sweet to the palate, one cannot make a meal of it." He paused before lowering his voice and continued, "Come home, my son, I miss you. I need you here."

Ahmed left on the next available flight to Baghdad a few days later. He arrived too late. A *Sunni* bomber had firebombed his father's house, and those who came to extinguish the flames never reached him on the top floor of their home. His father burned to death.

When Ahmed arrived at the horrific scene the next day, he asked why his crippled father was not saved. He was told by those in charge that there were holy books on the first floor which needed to be saved first. By the time that task was completed, the building was engulfed in flames, and his father had perished. Ahmed vowed his vengeance on all that day, vengeance against both the *Shiite* and the *Sunni*, and the governments that supported their terrorist's activities. His parents' deaths would be avenged. He vowed he would revenge the blood of his father and mother.

His plan for retribution took years to develop in his mind, and he knew he must be patient, but he was marked by the government as an outsider due to his Western education and prolonged overseas absences. In 2002, he could not find employment; worse, he was not allowed to leave the country. His friends deserted him, but he had plenty of time to think about the fate of his parents since he was penniless and had no place to live. He slept in deserted warehouses, homes, and office buildings. During the day, he begged for money, food; at night he searched for places to sleep, but he always remembered his pledge.

On March 20th, 2003, the Americans attacked the nation of Iraq and completely disabled and annihilated their infrastructure. The much-vaunted and feared army of Saddam's Iraqi regime wilted away and poured from the cities like sand into the desert.

The American military invaded, and after two weeks of minimal fighting, they overthrew the government of the dictator. But when the dust settled and when the American bureaucrats followed the troops they found a country without food, water, electricity, banks, schools, roads, military, or a police force to maintain order. Chaos, retribution, and looting were commonplace in the capitol. The country was on the verge of civil war or worse—anarchy. Something needed to be done and done quickly.

• • •

Ashton Jenkins, now a senior liaison representative with the State Department, landed in the desert capitol in May, 2003, shortly after the

American military took full control of the country. He arrived at the offices of The Iraqi Ministry of the Finance well after eleven P.M.

The offices were closed and had been for weeks. The only person Jenkins found there was Ahmed Koshari, sleeping on the floor of a storage room next to the minister's private office. It was dry, warm, and safe, and it was Ahmed's current, temporary home.

"You are with the finance ministry?" asked Jenkins of the rumpled Iraqi standing before him.

"Yes," responded the quick-thinking Ahmed. There was no longer a finance ministry in Iraq.

"I need someone in the ministry to help my government facilitate the transfer of American funds to help this country get back on its feet. Can you help me do this?" asked Jenkins, as he surveyed the man strangely dressed in rags standing in front of him.

Koshari rose to the occasion, brushed off his tattered clothes, and seized the opportunity before him.

Jenkins knew that the shortages were real in this country and overlooked the man's clothing. He was put at ease when the man responded in perfect English with a slight British accent.

The one thing the young Iraqi still had was his quick-thinking wit. "Yes, sir," he responded. "You have come to the right place. I am just the man to help you. I was working late tonight, in order to have things ready for your arrival, so please excuse my casual work clothes. My name is Ahmed, Ahmed Koshari. Welcome to Iraq."

They shook hands, and the deal was sealed. The largest transfer of funds in American history was about to take place and it was being overseen and coordinated by… Ahmed Koshari.

Chapter Five

Two weeks later on a bright May morning a nondescript tractor-trailer turned into the entrance of a partially hidden, three-story grey brick building at 100 Orchard Street in East Rutherford, New Jersey. The driver stopped at the entrance gate and, after being cleared by the armed security guard, proceeded to the plain structure beyond.

The building was hidden from the view of thousands of daily commuters by large trees and shrubs, but even if they paused to glance at the government building, they would not see the security cameras, infrared and motion sensors, or the patrolling rooftop sentries. They would, however, see one of the state police cars permanently stationed strategically at the front entrance. The building was the home of the East Rutherford Operations Center or more commonly referred to as EROC.

While the Federal Reserve's heart and brains were located thirteen miles away in Manhattan, the "wallet" was located here in this enormous storage building four times the size of the local Wal-Mart. In the surrounding middle-class neighborhood most people did not give it a second thought as they went about their daily lives. They would be surprised to know that here, just down the street from the neighborhood grocery store was a building more heavily protected than the gold depositary at Fort Knox. The fortress-like facility also had a state-of-the-art automated vault measuring two million cubic feet used for storing over sixty billion dollars of new and used U.S. currency.

The large semi-trailer backed into the shipping bay, and the driver remained in the cab of his truck. Inside the huge building, robotic arms shifted large blue shrink-wrapped "bricks" of cash onto pallets, preparing them for shipment to Iraq.

Each "brick" contained over $400,000 worth of one-hundred-dollar bills. Three supervisors and video cameras monitored the entire operation from above sitting behind bulletproof glass walls as they completed their paperwork. The money was retrieved from nearby money bays by robotic arms. It was then neatly arranged on vault tables before being loaded into automated retrieval vehicles then fed onto conveyors to the waiting tractor-trailer after exiting the shrink-wrapping process. During this entire process, the money was never touched by human hands.

When all of the money was loaded and accounted for, GPS devices were attached to the inside of the trucks doors then they were closed and sealed.

In all, twenty pallets of cash, weighing fifteen tons were loaded that day. Four hours later, the tractor-trailer turned back onto Route 17 and after three miles merged onto a southbound lane of the New Jersey Turnpike, looking like any other big rig on a busy highway before merging onto Interstate I-95 South.

Five hours later, the truck arrived at Andrews Air Force Base, outside Washington, D.C. There the seals on the truck were broken, and the cash was off-loaded and accounted for by Treasury Department auditors. The money was transferred to an army C-130 Hercules transport plane and ten heavily armed guards were posted throughout the plane. The next day, one billion, two hundred thousand American dollars arrived in Baghdad.

The money was unloaded from the plane by lift trucks and hauled to nearby warehouses for distribution. A portion of the cash made its way to the basement vault of the Central Bank of Iraq for allocation to government agencies. Some boxes of cash went the main office of the Coalition Provisional Authority, otherwise known as the CPA, while other containers of cash were sent to the many new ministries which distributed cash to pensioners, doctors, and other providers of essential services. Contractors were hired and paid to provide security and to maintain order in this rapidly unfolding "Wild West" arena.

When distributions were completed for the day, the bulk of the remaining mountains of cash were transported and stacked into warehouses at the nearby airport. The huge sliding door was then padlocked. One key was placed in the top desk drawer of Army Private First Class William Jones. He left every day at five o'clock and no guards were posted to secure the American-Iraqi cash trove. The other key to the lock was given to Ahmed Koshari, the new liaison between the Iraqi government and the coalition forces.

The trucks would return the following month and every month thereafter, and the whole procedure was replayed over and over again, filling more and more warehouses with an ever-expanding tsunami of cash. More warehouses were built to accommodate the mountains of cash. All of this was under the direct control of Ahmed Koshari. He was about to become a very busy and very, very wealthy man.

Chapter Six

The room in Baghdad was always crowded, full of American soldiers surrounded by large blue plastic "bricks" of cash shipped to Iraq to pay for the reconstruction effort. Each "brick" was worth over $400,000 in American greenbacks.

"So how much do you need this time?" the Army captain asked the old Iraqi standing before him. He had arrived like clockwork every month with his two sons for the last three years securing money for the payment of security forces in and around Baghdad.

"Thirty bricks. We had to hire more police and firefighters and then there is the tribute I have to pay to make sure I get through town without being blown up. You understand, I'm sure?"

"Yeah, yeah." He swung around in his chair, "Sergeant, give the man thirty bricks. Just sign the receipt roster here, Istaf," shoving a clipboard in front of him.

"Yousef, the name is Yousef."

"Yeah, yeah. Just sign here."

The small office was on the first floor of a three-story building inside the Green Zone in Baghdad. Piles of shrink-wrapped one-hundred-dollar bills were stacked high around the room. This cash distribution center was for the small projects while the larger projects were handled at the airport where cash could be distributed using pallet loads of blue shrink-wrapped American dollars.

As they were loading the van, which was parked outside, the captain asked, "So Istar, how many cops do we have on the payroll now?"

The old man stopped as he finished loading the cargo into the nearby truck, wiped his face with a worn handkerchief and said, "More than nine thousand now, but I am hiring more as we need them."

"I guess I'll need a roster sheet on who you've hired at some point. Just leave it on my desk inside when you put it together."

"Yes, captain."

The larger cash distributions at the airport were used to fund construction projects. The money was to rebuild the hospitals, schools, markets, water systems, and reconstruct damaged government buildings, the electrical grid, and everything else that had been destroyed in the brief war.

The tall American army officer looked outside at the long line of people waiting to come in; the hot noonday sun was already unbearable. The sweat dripped down his shirt, forming pools of moisture around his waist. He watched them standing there, waiting to fill their trucks and wheelbarrows with cash. The line stretched from his office, down the hall, out the door, and down the street, blocking traffic. Vendors were busy along the long line hawking their wares and selling food items and tea to the waiting residents of Baghdad.

"Enough. They'll just have to wait," the captain said to his new lieutenant fresh from the states. "Let's go have lunch. I'll let Ahmed handle it. I can trust him not to give away the store. Ahmed! Ahmed!" The young Iraqi appeared from nowhere.

"Yes, sir," he said, not looking up.

"Ahmed! We're going to lunch. I'm going to need a couple hundred bricks for tomorrow. When you get finished here, can you pick that up at the airport for me?"

"Yes, sir," the tall Iraqi responded.

"Thanks, Ahmed."

Ahmed, standing nearby, merely smiled in respect and nodded his head in agreement.

As the two military officers walked away towards the mess hall, the new arrival asked his captain, "You trust him with all that cash?"

The captain laughed, "Let me tell you about Ahmed. When we got our first shipment of cash, he was driving the transport truck with only one armed military guard inside the cab as his escort. Driving from the airport, down the dreaded 'Seven Mile Highway of Death,' he pulled to a stop to let an old man herd his sheep across the road. From nowhere two armed thugs jumped on the truck and shoved a pistol in his face and said, 'Drive! We won't kill you. We only want the money.'" The captain stopped and looked at his young companion, tossing his cigarette to the ground, putting it out under the toe of his boot.

"You see, the money, twenty million dollars in all, was in the rear of the truck. It was in batches of tens, twenties, and fifty-dollar bills. This was before the cash delivery production line had been refined to just use shrink-wrapped pallets of one-hundred-dollar bills," he chuckled.

"Well, Ahmed smiled, kept his cool and pulled out his forty-five caliber pistol and shot the man in the face as he pressed on the gas pedal and sped away. They never bothered our convoys again. Do I trust him? Yeah you bet, you see… it was me in that truck that day. I was the guard, and I was scared, scared shitless. He's one of the good guys. He's one of us. Believe me, you can trust him."

"You're kidding?"

"No, not at all. Besides when we have a problem that needs handling he's very resourceful. We had a stockpile of those depleted uranium shells that were driving our guys in the field crazy with nose bleeds, stomach ulcers, migraines, suicides, you name it. Well, we contracted with Ahmed to get rid of them. So, he gathers them up and flies them out of here and disposes of them. He also hauls the hospital radioactive waste for us. He saves us a big headache."

"What on earth does he do with it? Who's going to allow toxic depleted uranium shells and radioactive waste in their backyard? And wait, did you say he has his own planes? In wartime Iraq?"

"I don't ask. All I know is he gets the job done. I hear he just got some other passenger planes and flies regular service to bring in contractors and supplies. I also understand he has bought some old used oil tankers to ship out some of the oil we got flooding the fields everywhere. Since the oil wells are up and running, we got this stuff coming out of the ground and no place to put it, and it takes so much time to sell it. As I said, he's quite a resourceful guy. Don't sell him short. Oh and by the way he's also the main contact with the Northern Iraq Bank. We give them billions of cash every month. He personally oversees that they get their regular supply of money up north, hell, sometimes he even drives the trucks to the central bank himself. Hey, enough about Iraq, let's have some lunch, a beer, and then go watch some baseball."

"Sounds good to me. That Ahmed is some resourceful guy, very resourceful," he said muttering, turning to look over his shoulder at the young man dressed in Arab garb as they prepared to walk into the oasis of the nearly frigid mess hall. They heard a voice as they reached the steps.

"Captain, captain, please I must speak with you, please," said the old man in a ragged, torn suit, and shoes with no laces. His eyes were kind but imploring.

"Yes, what is it, Mustafa?"

"I need you sign document, captain. Please."

The young officer and his new companion looked over the old man and the paperwork he proffered to him. "Of course, Mustafa." The captain turned to the new arrival to explain. "He builds the hospitals and clinics here in Baghdad."

He reached for the paperwork and scrawled his signature then crossed out the amount and initialed it.

"But captain this clinic is only to cost one million dollars?" he said in broken English. "Here you wrote two million?"

"Yes, I know. Just give it to Ahmed and take your million. I'll take care of the other million later."

"Oh, I see," he said with a knowing smile, bowing as he retreated.

"What was that all about? And what's with the other million dollars?"

"MRA."

"What is that, MRA?"

"Well you've heard of IRA's right?"

"Yeah."

"Well MRA stands for My Retirement Account. It's for when I get the hell out of here and get back to the real world, just something to squirrel away for retirement. I'll teach you. Don't worry. We'll all go home wealthy men." They laughed walking into the officers' mess hall for lunch and to gain a respite from the boiling heat.

Ahmed stood there and watched them walk away. He returned to the old building to begin dispensing the piles of money stockpiled in the former Iraqi Ministry of Finance building. When he was finished, he again needed go to the airport and unlock one of the many warehouses filled with cash, load it on trucks, and bring it all back to Baghdad. Yes, that is exactly what he would do.

Chapter Seven

The tsunami of cash from the Federal Reserve to Iraq continued to arrive like clockwork every month for years. Towards the end of the war in Iraq a large delivery of cash arrived. The shipment was accompanied by the newly appointed Inspector General from Defense Contracting Audit Agency (DCAA), John Montage. He was there to finally do an audit on how the money had been spent. He was meeting with his old college roommate from Princeton University, four-star General Allen Wesley to discuss this and other issues with the theater commanding officer.

They sat down on dark leather chairs in the general's office with commendations and citations filling the paneled walls. "Still drinking bourbon and branch Jack?" The general asked.

"Yeah, but light on the bourbon... damn ulcers are killing me. I always thought I'd be dead from some sorry ass bullet," he laughed a painful and nervous laugh.

"I see you brought your whole goddamn accounting staff, Jack," quipped General Wesley, the American general in charge of the coalition in Iraq.

Now his old friend was not laughing. "Yes, I did." He lowered his voice, "Wes, I gotta level with you, the president is getting a lot of heat from Congress on both sides of the aisle as to what's happened to all the damn money we've been shoveling into this sinkhole. And the American people are getting hit with higher and higher gas prices week after week, and they want to know why and they're yelling for relief."

The general looked at his old friend saying, "Gas prices shouldn't be this high. We've been pumping oil faster and faster, but nothing seems to help. We're not making the money we thought we should be selling this oil. And we have the oil refineries and the ships operating at 100 percent, Jack. We got this oil everywhere."

His old friend took a sip from his glass and said, "Ships and oil supplies are turning up missing. For every tanker that is lost it increases the cost of gas in the U.S. by ten cents a gallon. Hell man, one of those tankers can carry enough oil to fuel an entire city in England for a day and now that oil is turning up missing. They carry upwards of two million barrels." His voice rose in pitch as the gravity of the situation began to sink in.

"I bet it's those goddamn hedge funds buying up oil futures betting that the price will go up."

"Well, whatever it is we have to get to the bottom of it. But I also want to show you another part of the problem." He reached into his briefcase and pulled out three pieces of paper. "See this?"

"Yeah, I see it. What is it?" asked the general, finishing off his scotch and pouring a refill for each of them.

"These three receipts, for purchase orders totaling over seven hundred million dollars! Did you hear me? I said seven... hundred... million dollars. Three damn pieces of paper. That is not Texas chicken feed my friend. No bids. No contracts. No other paperwork for spending seven hundred million dollars of the American taxpayers' money. I can't tell from this when this money was handed out, by whom, to whom, and for what. For all I know, it could have been to buy a small country. Damn it, Wes! And there's no accounting records for most of this stuff."

"Well Jack, you know this is a war zone. We did what we had to do and kept the paperwork for as long as we could then just got rid of it when we ran out of space. Or anytime we got a new commanding officer. Everybody wanted to clean up the paper trail before they left. You know how that goes," he said taking another sip of whiskey. His voice now had a nervous quiver to it. "That's just the way they have always done things here. Hell, I've only been here for nine months. You understand don't you?"

"No, I can't say that I do. You'll have a lot of explaining to do before Congress, my old friend. But before we go to dinner, I want to check out the cash reserves you have on hand at the airport."

General Wesley's eyes lit up. This is one thing he knew he had well under control. All of the extra cash was kept under lock and key in aircraft hangars at the airport. Billions upon billions were stored there. It was the only place it would be secure, that he was sure of. Besides he had Ahmed Koshari overseeing it.

The truck convoys pulled in front of the three massive aircraft hangars with dust rising up around them from all sides as they pulled to a stop.

"That hangar is where the cash comes in from the states," said Wesley pointing to the first building, "it's counted and then distributed to the Ministries, to the Iraqi National Bank, and the remainder is kept here for safekeeping. It's transferred from hangar one or hangar two as it comes in. Hangar three is the bank, as I like to call it. It's loaded to the rafters with cash," he said quietly. "And it's under lock and key at all times." He looked around for Ahmed. His Iraqi liaison should be here by now. He was getting nervous. Where the hell was he?

"Sergeant, where's Ahmed? I asked that he meet us here to answer any questions that the Inspector General may have."

"He has been out for the last couple of days," answered the old supply sergeant crisply before adding in a whisper, "I think he has a girlfriend on the side, somewhere outside of Bagdad that he likes to go visit. Not unusual for him lately. But don't worry, sir; I have the key to the bank." He lifted the padlock and inserted the key and with a click it sprang open. The muscular sergeant pushed open the huge hangar door and the crowd of men stood before the massive storage hangar, peering inside. It was totally empty. "Where's the money? Where's the goddamn money?" asked the general staring in disbelief. The money was gone, the oil tankers were gone and so were hundreds of millions of barrels of oil…and so was Ahmed. He was never seen in Iraq again.

• • •

Two weeks later, on the sundrenched island of Grand Cayman, a new hedge fund trader opened for business on the top floor of one of the most exclusive buildings on the island. The CEO and sole stockholder of Caribbean Island Trading Corporation was Ahmed Koshari. Within months, five oil-trading companies opened in New York, London, and the Caribbean. Their aim was to squeeze as much money as they could from oil-buying public while driving up the price of oil and making obscene profits. The race was on.

Chapter Eight

Nick Ryan loaded his Jeep and then was busy closing up the beach cottage in preparation for his trip to Key West. He was looking forward to it more then he thought. He had his letter of resignation from the Bureau on his desk. All he needed was to sign it and mail it to the FBI. Was it time for a new career? Could he fully devote all of his energies to the work he had once loved?

He was startled by the sound of his cell phone ringing. He still had a tough time getting used to the ring of his new cell phone.

"Hey, Pop," he said without looking at the caller ID. He liked life better before his present phone.

"Hey, Nicky. All packed?"

"Yep, just closing everything down."

His father paused for a moment before asking, "Did you mail the letter to the bureau?"

"No. Still thinking about it. Just not sure. I got six months to make up my mind."

"Well, if you want my opinion…"

"Pop, it's tough enough as it is. Please."

"Okay, Nicky. What else is bothering you? I can tell it in your voice."

"Still nothing about what happened to Del. None of my contacts at the agency have any news . Strange."

"At the bureau we all know that today could be our last. He was a good guy but it comes with the territory."

"Yeah, maybe you're right." Changing the subject he asked, "Dad, anything special you want for your birthday?"

"No, just have a good time and come back safe and sound. You could bring me a bottle of Jack Daniels when you come. I love you. Take care of yourself. You hear?"

"I hear you, Pop. See you in a week." The drive down the coast through the Keys over the bridges and past the crystal clear water was always relaxing. Hours later, he pulled onto Duvall Street and saw his gang of buddies waiting for him. For some reason, he had an unknown feeling of dread, which he could not shake since he left Delray. Something was wrong.

Chapter Nine

Ahmed Koshari stood in front of the tall office windows, which lined his twelfth-floor penthouse office suite overlooking the sunbathed city of Georgetown on the Grand Cayman Islands. He could look out over this thriving metropolis and see the dozens of buildings and businesses that he owned stretched out far beneath him. His holdings there and across the world were vast.

He had come a long way, he thought to himself, and the final pieces of his grand puzzle were about to fall into place. His father had always told him that revenge was sweeter with the passing of time. This dish he was about to serve would be very sweet.

Time was growing short, he thought. *I will have my revenge, and I will have it now.*

His breath grew shorter. Labored. He could not breathe. He loosened his two-hundred dollar Giorgio tie, but it did not help. He was choking. His voice searched for words, but they did not pass his lips. He tried to swallow. He coughed up blood.

"Mr. Koshari," came the voice of his assistant Lania, over the interoffice intercom, "your car is here to take you to the boat."

Ripping the buttons off his expensive cotton dress shirt he went to the bar at the other end of his office. He turned on the water, filled the basin and submerged his head while he sucked in huge quantities of liquid. For some reason that was the only thing that helped. The young Iraqi lifted his head and finally took in a deep breath. He looked into the mirror over the bar and saw his eyes were filled with blood, again. Blood trickled down his nose. The radium poisoning was taking its toll. The episodes were getting worse and more frequent. His left eye twitched uncontrollably.

"Mr. Koshari, Mr. Koshari?" came the voice again. "Is everything all right, sir?"

"Yes," he stammered, changing his shirt and tie. "I'll be right there." Blood still filled his eyes. He grabbed his sunglasses and made his way to his private elevator. He was not going to be late.

Chapter Ten

The aircraft, decked out in the New England Airways colors of gold and white, cranked the propellers causing the engines to cough blue and black smoke before springing to life. First, the right engines then the left. Soon both engines of the new Beechcraft airplane were humming in harmony. The smell of aviation fuel filled the air.

"NEA #634, you are cleared for takeoff. Please use runway one-niner. Have a good day NEA 634," came the call from the Boston control tower.

The takeoff was a textbook lift-off. The new plane quickly rose into the blue sky and began its fifty minute journey to the small city of Rutland, Vermont.

"Good morning folks," Captain Berger said over the intercom. "Welcome aboard New England Airways flight #634. We will be climbing to twenty-five thousand feet for our short hop from Boston to Rutland. I'll keep you updated as we approach our destination. Thank you for flying New England Airways. Please sit back and enjoy the flight."

Passenger and crew settled in for the short flight, observing the bucolic farms below as the plane climbed some fifteen thousand feet.

Boston tower did their routine handoff of NEA #634 to Rutland Control fifteen minutes later and now prepared to bring them in for a landing, just as they did every day for the past six months. Thirty minutes later, the co-pilot asked the passengers to buckle up their seatbelts as they prepared to land.

"Come in NEA 634, this is Rutland tower, we have you here. Welcome home. Bring your plane around to runway 22 and level off at 12,000 feet. We see you on our scope. Looking good, 634."

Senior air traffic controller, Gregory Linden was leading them home. He watched the plane make its course correction to prepare for their landing and saw a green dot blink on his screen. He watched the blinking light as he traced its path toward the airport. It was a smooth textbook landing. They should be within sight of the airport soon.

"Nice and steady, 634. Looking real good." *Two more hours then he could go home to his wife. He had the next two days off. Maybe we would go to—"* The green light went out. There was no blinking light on his screen. He stood from his seat and looked in the direction of the plane. No lights! Then he saw something that gave him a sickening feeling in his gut, a fireball appeared off in the hills to the east. It was New England Airways flight #634.

Chapter Eleven

In the 1980s, Kowlooni Wie had travelled constantly from Shanghai, China, to Mexico City setting up new routes to ship cocaine from China to the United States. He was ruthless in dealing with his drug competitors in the Mexican capitol, as headless corpses filled the empty lots in the suburbs surrounding the city. His business was booming.

One day in a local Mexico City restaurant he was smitten by the young Mexican waitress who waited on him and his associates. Wie was used to getting everything he wanted, and within weeks the pretty teenage waitress with smiling brown eyes was living with him in his walled compound. She soon bore him two children, Javier and Maria.

The oldest child, Javier was extremely shy and originally thought to be mute since he rarely spoke, even in school. He was large and powerfully built for his age but soon found he was ostracized by his Mexican friends because of his prominent Asian features. His classmates made fun of him and called him "Chino."

At age sixteen, one of his father's drug rivals, a Frenchman named Philippe Montserrat, killed both of parents in a car bombing. Fearing retribution from the big brooding teenager, the Frenchman put out a contract on the remaining family members. Javier and his sister fled on a freighter bound for Miami to live with a distant relative.

To survive, the teenager went to work for a local roofing company. In South Florida, the roofs are weighted down with thousands of heavy concrete roof tiles. Javier soon became a local legend, lifting twenty of the heavy roof tiles on his shoulders, twice that of other workers. His shoulders were broad, and his back became strong as he toiled in sweltering heat of the South Florida sun.

Chino insisted his younger sister continue her education and with the money he earned he enrolled her in a local private high school. The pretty girl with the beautiful smile and long black hair stole the hearts of all the boys at school. One day walking home, she was offered a ride home in an older classmate's new car. He tried to assault her, but she defended her virtue. To teach her a lesson, he slashed her face repeatedly with his knife.

Chino's was out of control with rage when he saw what happened to his precious little sister. He vowed revenge.

The local police cautioned him that the young man Javier suspected of the crime was from a good upstanding family and not possible it was him and that it would be unwise for him to pursue any further action against him. The police threw Chino in jail for two days to cool him down before releasing him with a warning. Upon his release he learned from the hospital that his sister could not bear to live with such disfigurement and had jumped off the roof, killing herself.

One week later newspapers reported that the son of a prominent businessman in Miami was missing, presumed kidnapped. Javier was taken in for questioning but released some twelve hours later when they could not charge him with anything. Soon, parts of the dismembered, tortured body of the young man began appearing across the city over the weeks that followed. The final private pieces were found by the young man's father, wrapped inside the family's Sunday morning newspaper.

Months later, Chino was attacked in an elevator by five men intent on killing him, but he was the only one to survive the encounter when it reached the basement floor garage. He felt the powerful adrenalin rush from those killings and decided that is what he did best. Javier was bright, methodical, and patient—all the skills needed for a top assassin—and soon became feared throughout the barrios of Miami.

Two years later Javier Wie disappeared into the night and soon was known only as "Chino," the dreaded and feared shadowy contract killer. His skills and reputation were known worldwide. By the year 2014, he was the best—but only if you could afford it.

Chapter Twelve

The maroon drapes behind the desk rustled briefly, as he came into the room and sat behind his computer. He set down his cold drink and typed an e-mail to his brother-in-law, Nick Ryan.

Nick—
OK, OK, you win. I'll come to Florida for your next damn fishing trip.
Seriously though, thanks for asking, again. See ya soon.
Love ya,
Tony
P.S. I still miss her too—every day.
T

Anthony Galvechio paused for a few moments, an old accounting habit, before deciding to hit the send button on his e-mail to his brother-in-law Nick. What the hell he thought, go for it. It'll be fun. *He had not seen Nick since Katie's funeral, and his brother-in-law was always inviting him down to Florida for fishing visits. He liked Nick, always had liked him, and besides he hadn't taken any time off from his job at the Defense Contract Audit Agency (DCAA) in years.* What the hell, *he hit the send button.*

His smile faded immediately as he regretted his decision and looked at the pile of paperwork on his desk and other papers and boxes scattered about the floor in his home office. He had equal amounts of work waiting for him at the agency. Both offices smelled of stale paper and cardboard boxes. When would he ever get it all done, he asked himself?

The balding, middle-aged bachelor took another drink from his chilled, sweating glass of Jack and ginger, almost finishing the glass. Unloosening his tie, he reached for the familiar bottle of Jack Daniels, which kept him company at his desk every night. The hell with the ginger ale he thought and poured himself another tall one. He took a large, loud drink. He knew he could work for hours even after filling and refilling his glass multiple times. Besides he would double- and triple-check everything before submitting his report on Friday.

His eyes squinted as he looked at the computer screen and then removed his glasses. *Hell, it's only ten o'clock. I can't be getting sleepy already. There's still a lot to do.*

He had arrived home from the office an hour earlier and wanted to get right to work and delve into the large briefcase he had brought home. The four other worn brown leather briefcases waited for him against the wall as they yearned for his attention, but tonight he was going to focus on the one he brought home that day. The others would have to wait for another time.

Tony noticed at the agency that something simply did not add up, and to an auditor that was the kiss of death. Everything had to add up. He brought the paperwork home to study it further. Tony was the best the agency had on the job; he would get to the bottom of it.

He took a bite of his leftover tuna fish sandwich on white bread that he bought for lunch that day and felt the soggy bread soak into his fingers. He tossed the mushy sandwich onto the plate. It landed next to the red Jonathan apple he bought on the way home. It was then he noticed a blue sheet of paper lying at the side of his desk, just beyond the phone.

Reaching for it he began to read,

To Whom It May Concern…

His eyes grew weary again—he squinted. *I need my damn glasses, that's what I need.* He picked them up and refocused his attention once more,

To Whom It May Concern:

Please do not think ill of me for that is not my intent. I only wish to say my goodbyes…

Laying the paper down on his desk, he leaned back in the old green leather chair he bought years earlier at a local flea market. He lowered his whiskey glass to the desktop and unbuttoned the top button of his white dress shirt to get some air. The room began to spin; it was no use … he could not keep his eyes open. His head hit the desk with a loud thud—he was out.

The drape behind him moved again and a tall, patient figure dressed in black to blend in with his surroundings, stepped out. The big man pulled the accountant's head back slowly from the desktop until it rested on the back of his chair. He retrieved the revolver from his pants pocket, positioned it in the drugged man's right hand, placed the muzzle to his temple, and pulled the trigger.

The blast was thunderous but gone in an instant. A blue powdery haze hung in the air. One bullet was all that was needed to do the job. Tony was dead. The left side of the government accountant's skull was shattered from the wound, blood sprayed in all directions.

Chino moved with purpose, dropping the gun to the floor beneath the dead man's hand. He paused and took a moment to survey the room and then picked up the large oversized briefcase on the floor beside the dead man's desk. Stopping for a brief moment to retrieve the apple from the plate he took a large bite and walked out the same way he entered, through the rear kitchen door.

Once outside, Chino passed the rear yards of the quiet suburban neighborhood and tossed the half-eaten apple core over a nearby fence.

He walked slowly but steadily down the dimly lit alleyway so he looked like he belonged in the neighborhood until he reached his car parked at the end of the street. The neighborhood dogs did not bark at the loud noise nor did they seem even notice him as he walked by them in the dark. The assassin removed his gloves, turned them inside out, and shoved them into the plastic bag he carried in his pants pocket. He had what he came for; his assignment was done.

Chapter Thirteen

Sean Kenyon nearly missed the sign off to the side of the old dirt road, having only the cloudy moonlight to guide his way towards the Valley of the Macoute. *He turned off onto a one-lane path marked only with a faded* Gauloises French *cigarette ad posted to the side of an old red roadside shack. He was beginning to rethink the wisdom of coming out in the middle of Jamaican mountain wilderness at such a late hour. The road ended abruptly some three hundred yards from where he had turned off.*

Sean Kenyon was an independent stringer for the *Saint Louis Herald* newspaper and was following up on a lead on a story he had been developing without telling anyone. He wanted all of the credit. It was going to be big, really big. If only he could land just one major story, he knew the newspaper would have to hire him full time. He'd show them what he was made of, that he was sure of.

Since all the costs were coming out of his pocket, the young would-be investigator checked into the cheapest hotel he could afford, the *Little Jamaica Hotel* on a side street in downtown and snapped a picture of the façade with his cell phone. The room was adequate but without air conditioning, it was stifling at night in the steamy summer sun of Little Jamaica. The ceiling fan hung down low above his bed but provided little relief. The daily rains only made it worse.

Next, he arranged for a rental car he could drive to an area far beyond the city limits and asked for directions to the Macoute Valley at the hotel. An old hunchbacked cleaning woman told him, "Mon, you no go near that valley. Macoute territory is bad magic, bad voodoo. Beware, Mon, of… Catawampus! Tiger eyes!" she muttered on, as if she were trying to bless him to fend off the danger of the unknown.

Her daughter joined in, "They are devils that sting and have yellow eyes that glow in the dark. Stay away from them, mon," cautioned the frightened young teenager. The fear showed in their eyes.

Sean had heard the wives' tales spread by local wealthy landowners meant to keep the prying eyes of locals away from their big lavish waterside estates. But he had a story to track down and no bogeyman was going to stop him.

An older, distinguished-looking local Brit, sitting nearby, gave him directions but also told him to be very careful between gulps of his Scotch whiskey. Sean needed the pictures of the mansion for his story; he had to go, he had no choice.

He parked the car by some underbrush and walked down the path just wide enough to accommodate two people. It soon ended at a fence over fifteen feet high topped with barbed wire. He shined his flashlight on a metal sign hanging from the fence commanding:

NO TRESPASSING
KEEP OUT!
CATAWAMPUS

At the bottom of the sign was the figure of skull and crossbones. The sign confirmed it; he was at the right place.

Using techniques he had learned when he was in the Marine Corps, he nimbly hoisted himself up and over the fence, then back down the other side. He began making his way forward again as the path became wider, with less trees but more shrubs everywhere. In the moonlight, he could see the lights from the house in the distance.

"Phew, what died here?" he asked softly to himself, encountering an unbearable stench. It smelled of sulfur and something else—death. He heard a rustle of leaves off to his left and shined his flashlight into the bushes. Orange eyes, low to the ground, glared back at him from the darkness. The eyes charged at him.

Sean took off running at full speed and could hear whatever was behind the orange yellowish eyes chasing him, their noise getting closer. His breathing was deeper now. Closer, they were getting closer. He could hear them right behind him. He tossed his camera bag back at them to try to slow them up. They kept chasing.

In front of him he saw more eyes coming towards him. Scared, he ran to the right to get away from the oncoming danger and felt something lunge at him, biting him, nipping at his leg as he ran. The gash stung as he felt warm blood oozing down his leg. They howled to signal the others to join in the chase.

Sean thought he heard voices ahead and saw a flashlight. He saw lights ahead illuminating the night and the huge white mansion at the top of a small hill in front of him.

He knew he had to make it there and heard the pack of the orange and yellow-eyed creatures chasing him. Suddenly in front of him was another fence similar to the one he had just climbed. But this fence had a sign with the picture of a lightning bolt affixed to the fence. An electrified fence. *Aw, shit!*

They were right behind him, and he heard more coming from his left while others were charging at him on the right. A set of sharp teeth sank deep into his leg, and excruciating pain shot through his body. His brain registered white pain, as the teeth fastened their grip, and it was then he heard his leg being crushed, snapped and broken like it was a twig. The pain was unbearable. Blood was rushing from the wound making them growl and gnarl all the louder. The scent of blood was in the air, and they went crazy. They would not be denied their prey.

The young would-be reporter now stood, hobbling on one leg. He turned to face them, and all he could make out was a sea of orange and yellow eyes slowly advancing towards him. He stepped back closer to the fence, so close he thought he could hear the electric current humming through it.

The bright set of eyes closest to him jumped and grabbed his arm, ripping the flesh before letting go. They smelled and had tasted blood.

He yelled at them, and they stepped back but did not retreat. *His mind was in a twisted survival mode. Maybe he was wrong, maybe the fence wasn't electrified?* He had no choice; the pack was coming in for the kill. He turned and jumped at the fence in an effort to climb it. His camera, a graduation present from his older sister, slipped from his hands and spiraled to the grass below, hitting one of them, causing a howl.

The putrid smell of sizzling flesh filled the night air and the orange eyes sat, waiting for their dinner to fall to the ground. The electronic monitoring gauges in the house showed a power drop in sector sixteen. That was the only indication that young Sean Kenyon was gone. The army of orange eyes howled with pleasure in the night. Tonight was a good night.

Chapter Fourteen

"Come on, Ryan. Put your back into it! Come on you can do it!" They all joined in the shouting. Nick Ryan was strapped into the fighting hot seat of the fishing charter boat Lady Luck.

The boat was owned by former Chicago police captain Denny Rollins, and it was always fully booked for the fishing season with cops coming to Key West to enjoy some sport fishing. Today was no exception. It was every cop's dream to retire to Key West and buy a charter boat or open up a bar. Denny did just that.

"Damn it, Ryan, keep that line tight," he screamed from lookout post above. He re-positioned the boat to maintain the distance with the fighting fish and keep the line taut.

"Come on, you can do it! That's it!" chimed in the rest of the guys on the charter boat. They continued to watch him reel the fish in, urging him on. He had been battling the hellish fish for over forty-five minutes, but the fighter gave no signs of giving up.

"Pull the damn thing up so we can at least see what the hell you've hooked. He looks too big for a dolphin, too small for a shark but he sure fights like hell!" screamed Mike Mansfield, chief of police at the Delray Beach police department.

"Whatever you do, don't lose him!" ranted the old Scotsman.

"There," shouted Mark Parker, "There he is! Shit! Oh my God, you hooked a 'cuda! A big one!"

The fish broke the surface just long enough to be identified; its angry eyes told everyone on the boat it was no fish to be trifled with in these cold blue waters. Nobody liked to mess with a barracuda. Its skin was cursed and thought to be toxic, but they gave one hell of a fight when hooked.

Ryan's muscular arms strained to hold the massive fighting fish in check. His t-shirt was soaked with sweat from the ordeal, but he was no closer to bringing the fish in close enough to the boat to gaff him.

"Just fight 'em Nicky, don't bring it aboard. Can't eat 'em. Bad stuff but a helluva fighter. Just bring him close," directed Parker.

"Cuda's are bad luck," seconded the Captain.

After another twenty minutes, the struggling fish came alongside the charter boat. It was a beauty.

"Wow! That's a one-fifty pounder if it's is an ounce, that's for sure," shouted the captain. He cut the leader line, and the barracuda swam away to fight another day.

"Beers on you tonight, Ryan. You got the record so you get to buy the first round."

His back was sore from the fight, but he loved arranging these monthly fishing outings for all the guys. It was like being a cop again. It was on days like this, with the good-natured camaraderie and kidding that made him almost regret his thoughts about leaving the agency.

"We'll eat well tonight at The Mermaid," Nick shouted. The Blue Mermaid was his favorite restaurant and whiskey bar in Key West. They had caught a dozen cobia, pompano, and mahi throughout the day but Ryan's barracuda catch would be the talk of the night. It was also the heaviest. Ryan smiled.

"Hey guys, I have a favor to ask." He sat on the boat hatch sipping a beer. "If you guys don't mind... I've invited my brother-in-law Tony to join us next month on our fishing trip. He's not a cop, but I've been after him for years to come to Florida and he's finally agreed."

"Sure, I got no problem with him joining us," said Mike, "As long as he likes to fish, drink beer, and as long as he plays poker poorly." The rest nodded in agreement.

"Well, one out of three ain't bad," responded Nick as the boat neared the dock. It had been a good day, but Nick was happy to be back heading to shore.

Nick would drive home up the coast highway to Delray in the morning and have dinner with his father that night. Ryan had moved in with his dad at his beach house in Delray a year earlier. He moved from Baltimore after his wife died, and he decided he needed a change of scenery and not a place filled with so many memories. There were just too many reminders in Baltimore. No sooner did he get to Florida that his Dad underwent surgery. The old charmer, approaching seventy, moved in with his nurse after he was discharged. *Some guys just knew how to live.*

Seagulls and pelicans circled the incoming fishing boat waiting for the discards from the pier as the catch of the day was cut, filleted, and cleaned. They knew they could count on filling their bottomless bellies with the leftovers of the day. They staked their claim ashore, perched on top of the pilings waiting their turn.

"Hey Nick," hollered Jerry West, "tell your brother-in-law to bring plenty of cash for our next fishing trip. We'll be happy to take everything he's got and…" his jeer was interrupted by Nick's cell phone jangling in his pocket. Nick held up his hand while he took the call.

He looked at the caller ID; it was his dad. "Hey Pop, I was just getting ready to call you. We just pulled in to Key West. We made a good catch today. I got some nice pompano for you and Michelle. You're going to love—"

"Nick," his father started, sounding serious, "Tony's dead."

"What?" Nick shouted in disbelief. "I just got an email from him before I came down here. He said he was lookin' forward to coming here for my next fishing outing. I can't believe it. I just can't."

"He committed suicide two days ago. I was planning on flying up to D.C. for his funeral and figured you would probably want to go. I booked us on a one o'clock flight for tomorrow."

"Of course I want to go. I'll come back early, drive back tonight, and pick you up tomorrow at home before the flight. God Pop, I don't understand. I just talked to him a week ago, and he sounded fine." *What the hell is going on here? First Del, now Tony. Shit- this can't be happening.*

"Nick are you there?" he heard his father say on the other end of the phone.

"Yeah, I'm here Pop."

"I can't believe it either. But listen, that's just the way things are sometime son. I gotta go. I am going to go and get drunk with Michelle. He was a good soul. See ya tomorrow, Nicky."

"Bye, Pop. See ya. Love ya."

"Love ya too, son."

The five-hour drive home that night on the darkened two-lane Ocean Highway gave Nick a lot of time to think about Tony and the times they shared together. He had one hand on the wheel, and his mind was lost in foggy thoughts. Tony was the only family that his wife Katie had, and now he was gone too. His thoughts drifted to his Katie.

He had solved her murder and finally had some closure, but there was not a day that went by that he didn't miss her. He remembered how she laughed; her nose would crinkle, her eyes would light up, and the laugh would come flowing out of her, almost like a prayer. He was lost in her, the thoughts of her still drove him crazy and how he wished she—

Wake up! He heard her voice scream. He looked up. The semi-trailer was heading right at him. He could see the headlights flashing, blinding him. He jerked the wheel. *Pull to the right. Harder! Both hands. Hard. Harder!*

Nick narrowly averted a head-on collision with the huge eighteen-wheeler. He was close enough that he could see the angry face of the truck driver as he passed by, blasting him with his booming air horn. It pierced the still night on the dark Florida Keys Highway. *That was close.* He didn't ask about where the saving voice came from, he knew. *Stay awake, stay alert. Thanks, Katie.*

It was late when he pulled his Jeep onto the gravel driveway, opened the double wooden garage doors and parked his Jeep next to his wife's vintage ailing Porsche. He had driven her car down from Baltimore after her funeral and as soon as he parked it in the garage at the beach cottage, it expired. He was still working on it to help try to revive it, but so far it was no use. Now it was just covered by a painter's old grey drop cloth waiting for Nick to finish the job.

He was glad to be home, and after taking a quick shower he grabbed a bottle of whiskey from the liquor cabinet and sat down behind his computer and reread his recent e-mail message from Tony. His message didn't sound like someone about to commit suicide. He would have to investigate that quietly on his own. He was puzzled. *Something just didn't make sense.*

A picture of him and Katie at the beach sat on his desk, a constant reminder of how much he missed her. He picked it up, smiled, and said, "You saved my life tonight, kiddo. You know that, don't you? I love you more now than ever before."

He gently kissed her photo and set the picture frame back on his desk. It had been a long drive back from the Keys. The fiery whiskey felt smoother as he finished the bottle. His eyelids drooped as he fell asleep caressing her with his mind. The bottle hit the floor with a thud rolling towards his sofa.

The next morning he was still seated at the table; he had overslept. A pasty, clammy whiskey taste filled his mouth. Nick showered, threw on some clothes, gulped down a quick cup of coffee while he toasted an English muffin and grabbed his packed suitcase. As he flung open his front door to leave, before him stood a longhaired woman with her back to him.

When he opened the door, she spun around and there she stood—it was his Katie!

Chapter Fifteen

Her hair was somewhat darker, slightly longer, and her face thinner, but she was still as beautiful as ever. The beautiful emerald green eyes, which spoke so many languages, were there, smiling, laughing, but now with only a hint of recognition.

Nick's mouth dropped, his stomach heaved, and his legs shook, as he stood there defenseless. He didn't know what to say or do. *Calm down. Hold on.* He tried to compose himself. *Katie's gone, remember? Or is she?* Standing there before her, without saying a word, his mouth open, staring at her was all he could do. *It can't be her. Or is it? Maybe, maybe life is fair after all?*

"Katie?" he implored his eyes still fixed on her.

"Nick?" she asked in that oh-so-familiar voice in a slightly higher tone then he expected.

"Yes…"

She paused, "Are you Nick, Nick Ryan?" she asked again.

Standing there frozen, he could not power his brain to move his tongue to respond to her. He just stood there, mesmerized. *Katie! It can't be. But she was standing there, right in front of him.* He wanted to throw his arms around her—but something stopped him.

"Hi," she said, showing her discomfort at being stared at by him. "I was looking for Nick Ryan," she asked. Her voice was only slightly different, maybe softer then Katie's.

"I'm… Nick…" he finally stammered like a schoolboy, unable to take his eyes off of her. She had the same easy smile, the same beguiling dimple on her cheek. Yes, it had to be Katie, but that was not possible. Katie had been brutally murdered two years earlier. He wanted to rush and hold her, kiss her and never ever let her go again. Oh my God, she had Katie's captivating eyes, piercing eyes, the eyes that said come here. At least that's the way Nick read them. He was enthralled by the dark-haired beauty with round beautiful eyes and a smile that he could never say no to. He stepped towards her.

Unprepared, she moved backwards.

Nick, finally recovered, cleared his voice and said, "Yes…, yes, I'm Nick," he responded as if he won a lottery prize.

"We don't know each other …but I got your name from a friend of mine, Mike Marshall, Chief of Military Protocol at the military clinic I work at in Boca Raton. He said I should talk to you." She paused for a moment before she continued. "Is there something going on that I am not aware of?"

Nick stammered to his senses, *This can't be Katie, but my God she looks and sounds just like her.* "I'm sorry. You just look very familiar. You remind me of someone that's all. I'm sorry. I don't mean to stare. For a moment there I thought you were…somebody else." He was interrupted by his cell phone and its insistent ring emanating from his pocket. "Excuse me for a moment, will you please?" It was his dad.

"Hey, Pop. Can I call you back?"

"No! Nicky, we're late! Come on, we're going to miss our flight. We should be at the airport by now, and you haven't even picked me up yet. What the hell's going on?"

"Sorry, Pop. I'm leaving now. Be there soon."

"Get your ass in gear. Ummh…damn kids…" Nick could hear his father's voice trail off as he ended the call.

Nick turned and could not believe she was standing there in front of him. He set his luggage on the ground.

She smiled a sweet smile and said, "My name is April Kenyon, Doctor April Kenyon. I need to hire a private investigator to find my brother who's turned up missing. Mike thought you might be just the person to help me. He knows your dad, Frank."

Nick studied her face, a new face but one he had known his whole life. *God, she's beautiful.*

Nick's dad, Frank Ryan, had been with the FBI over twenty-eight years before a gunshot and surgery pushed him into early retirement. Everybody knew Frankie. He didn't slow down after retirement and still turned the head of all the pretty nurses at his rehab facility, until moving in with his former nurse, Michelle.

"I was just on my way out the door to pick him up. I'm sorry, but I'm late for a flight. We leave this morning for Washington, D.C., to attend a funeral tomorrow." Nick closed the beach cottage door behind him and joined her on the porch of the old house. He wished he could stay and help her. Maybe when he got back in town.

Her voice quivered. "Mr. Ryan, I have nowhere else to turn. Sean is the only family I have left in the world."

"Walk with me to my car," he told her. "Tell me all you know. Maybe I can help when I get back in town. I'm only gone for a few days."

They walked down the steps, where he lifted the old wooden garage door and tossed his things into the rear of the Jeep.

"I don't know much," she began. "My brother, Sean Kenyon, is a freelance reporter for the *Saint Louis Herald*. He told me he was working on a big story about government abuse when he called me to say it has turned out to be a much bigger story than even he had ever imagined. He was keeping everything hush-hush like he always does and didn't tell me much. Sean said he was on his way to somewhere in the Caribbean, but that was over two weeks ago and neither I nor his fiancée have heard from him since."

Caribbean?

"Maybe he's just enjoying the sun and beach on the islands. He'll turn up, I'm sure of it," Nick responded, trying to sound reassuring.

"No, this isn't like him, and besides he's scheduled to get married soon and we haven't heard from him. I am afraid something terrible has happened." Her voice fluttered. "Mr. Ryan, have you ever lost someone you loved, I mean really loved? He's the only family I have. I must find him."

The words ripped through him like a dagger, piercing his heart. His thoughts went back to his Katie and how he felt when she was taken from him. He was confused. His Katie was gone but here she was, back, standing in front of him, nearly in tears and asking for his help. What else could he do?

"I'm sorry, Mr. Ryan. I didn't mean to say that. Please forgive me. I'm just desperate and have nowhere else to turn. And worse, I leave to go out of town later today." She paused, looking down at his suitcase, "But I see you're very busy; I'll let you go. I don't want you to miss your flight." She looked at him, her eyes searching his face then said, "Goodbye, Mr. Ryan." She turned and walked away.

Nick watched her and then ran to catch up with her. "Wait," Nick shouted after her. He wasn't going to lose her again. "Do you have a recent picture of your brother?"

April turned back to face him; a ray of hope lit her face. "Yes, yes I do. I can forward one to you from my phone or... wait I think I have one in my purse." She fumbled in her large handbag and pulled out a picture of herself and her brother sitting next to one another on a catamaran on the beach. She had on a two-piece swimsuit, which she filled out nicely, but he wisely said nothing. Her swimsuit was cut low. *God was she built,* just like he remembered. He glanced at his watch, he was late. *Shit!* His timing was always off, he thought to himself.

"Listen…," trying to remember her name.

"April, April Kenyon," she said, her voice cracking.

"Listen, April. My clients are usually only insurance companies, and normally I don't do missing persons. I'll be gone for a couple of days in D.C. for a funeral. I'll look into it and see what I can find out. But I'll help you under two conditions."

She nodded her head.

"One, let me borrow this picture and I'll make some inquires and see what I can find out. But no promises okay?"

She nodded her head vigorously. "OK," she said, seemingly happy for a glimmer of hope.

Nick slid inside the Jeep and she came nearer, closing the car door and leaning up against it. She now managed what could pass for a faint smile. As she leaned against the car door, her blouse was partly open. Trying not to notice he could not help but see her womanly charms in the flesh.

"You said two conditions. What is the second condition?"

"The other condition," he told her as he started the car, "is that you call me Nick. My dad is Mr. Ryan. OK?"

The half-smile bloomed into a grin across her face. "I'm sorry Nick, but Sean is the only family I have left, and I'm real worried about him," she said.

"Give me a number where I can reach you. Can I call you when we both get back in town? Then you'll have my undivided attention."

"Promise?"

"I promise."

She handed him her business card and scribbled her cell phone across the bottom. "Call me day or night if you find out anything. I'm scheduled to be out of the country for a while, but you can always leave me a message."

"OK. Are you sure your husband or boyfriend won't get mad if a strange man calls?"

"I'm no longer married, and I don't have a boyfriend." She smiled.

"You said you're out of the country for a while? That sounds mysterious."

"No, you see I'm a military doctor, and you know how that can be. I'm stationed at a military rehab clinic in Boca Raton, but I still travel quite a bit. But I shouldn't be gone long." She paused before continuing, "Nick, I must ask you, have we met before? You know in the sunlight you look so familiar."

Not really knowing what to say he mumbled, "We met in another life," before changing the subject. "Anything else you can tell me about your brother?"

"The only other thing I can think of is right before we lost contact with him I got a text message from him. It was strange, it was just one word."

"What was it?"

"Catawampus."

Chapter Sixteen

Tuesday morning the two young sisters, Ashura, twelve years old, and Mali, thirteen, walked together down the streets of Taji in Northern Iraq. They held hands as they walked; they talked and giggled about their little secret. They both wore the traditional clothes expected of young girls in conservative Iraq. Two silver coins jingled in their pockets.

The young girls covered themselves with the *abayah*, a long black cloak worn over a dress which went from head to toe, the *asha*, a black head scarf and a *foota*, a black chin scarf. They were dressed as seventy-year-old widows based on Western standards, but they thought nothing of it as it was the uniform of every girl and woman in Iraq once they left their homes.

They walked along the streets, young boys taunted them as they passed by the gutted and bombed-out buildings. They were not tempted; they were on their way to heaven.

The sentry, a young American GI, along with a military Iraqi interpreter, stopped them at a security checkpoint.

"Where are you going?" they asked

"To school."

"What school? There are no girls' schools around here."

"Al Shaebab," they answered in unison.

"Why this way? That school is blocks from here, on the other side of those buildings," asked the suspicious Iraqi, pointing over to the west. "This is a secured zone, along with military and police training here. Go away! Go home."

"It is too dangerous for us to travel the other roads to get to our school. There are too many bombers, please? Please let us through," the older one pleaded in perfect English.

The young American soldier smiled and said, "Let 'em pass. It's OK. They won't harm anybody."

The girls smiled at the cute young American soldier, tall, blond hair with his shiny white-toothed smile. They all looked the same to the young girls as they waved goodbye and walked down the street. Soon, the girls passed by a large field which was a soccer field prior to the invasion but now served as a refueling depot for the Americans and the Iraqis. The smell of gasoline and diesel fuel filled the dusty air. Iraqis renamed the temporary base *Karem Safin*. It was a large repair facility and served as an enormous fuel depot area for the American and Iraqi military. Giggling, the young girls could see the huge gasoline storage tanks behind the trucks and artillery vehicles.

The young girls walked past a young Iraqi sentry who was texting his girlfriend and headed towards the many gasoline tankers located at the center of the field. As they neared the trucks a crowd of young soldiers stopped them and soon encircled the girls, taunting them, jeering at them in their own familiar way.

"Where are you two princesses going?" asked a dark-haired Iraqi sergeant. "Does the king know his young princesses are gone from his home?"

"Does he know that they are alone and out, unescorted by a male relative?" the oldest one asked.

As the crowd surrounding them grew larger, soldiers stopped their duties, joined them, and now laughed at the girls who clung to each other in fear.

"I will see you in heaven," said the oldest, being the first to pull her hand from her sleeve. Her hand held down a switch. Both she and her sister released the button at the same time. The huge explosion killed all eighty soldiers and civilians surrounding them. The secondary explosion from the nearby gasoline supply storage tanks shook the earth. The resulting fireball could be seen for miles. Other, multiple explosions reverberated in rapid succession around the city. The shrill pleading of the sirens of the dispatched fire trucks and ambulances broke the air of complacency of the city as the emergency vehicles rushed to survey the carnage.

After the explosion confirmed that his handiwork was done, the man in the tan Peugeot sedan drove the car away from the curb on the side street and headed towards the airport. The middle-aged, balding man, nicknamed "Mr. Tuesday," was on his way back to Baghdad. He was one of fifteen "Mr. Tuesdays" traveling throughout the country bombing and enlisting support for the cause of the righteous.

His work here was done. In the capital city, everything would be ready for him. He had a week before his next mission, but tomorrow was Wednesday in Northern Iraq and time for others to create havoc.

Chapter Seventeen

Nick Ryan pulled the Jeep from the garage and shoved her card into his pocket. Catawampus? *He had never heard the word before. Using his phone at a stoplight, a quick check of the internet shed little details on the word. To the side, crooked, awkward? Fierce animal—bogeyman.* Hey, this phone is handy after all, *he thought to himself. He would definitely look into her brother's disappearance. He wanted to have something to report when he saw her next.* God, how he wished he did not have to go Washington for the funeral. But it was his duty; it was his brother-in-law and a good friend.

April Kenyon, the name just rolled from his lips. Soon a twinge of guilt crept into his thoughts. *What about Katie? What would his Katie want?*

"Where the hell you been?" his father's voice shook him back to reality as he pulled in front of Michelle's house. "We're going to be late, and if you make me miss this flight, Nicky, there's going to be hell to pay."

Nick knew better to respond to his dad when he was this angry. They made it to the airport in record time.

"Follow me," said the elder Ryan, flashing his retired FBI credentials at security, bypassing the line of weary travelers waiting their turn. "He's my son," pointing behind him over his shoulder in Nick's direction before he could produce his own badge.

"We'll never make it," said Nick breaking out into a trot as they headed down the hallway to their gate.

"Here we are, Gate 17."

A pretty airline stewardess stood at the top of the gangway waving to them as they approached. "You must be the Ryans? Right this way, gentlemen. We upgraded you to first class. Please, follow me."

"Thank you," said the older Ryan in his most gracious tone. "We appreciate that and so does the president."

"The president?" Nick said under his breath in wonderment.

"Well, I had to do something," whispered the senior Ryan. "I sure the hell didn't want to miss this flight and be late for the funeral."

They settled into the large, comfortable first-class leather seats, which made a loud poof noise as they sat down. The flight was a little over two hours long and before Frank drifted off to sleep, Nick asked him, "Hey Pop, have you ever heard of the term, catawampus?"

"Well, let me think." He adjusted his pillow. "I think it means crooked or maybe… I'm not sure, but I think it also has another evil or darker meaning. Why do you ask?"

"Well, part of the reason I was late today is as I was leaving the house a woman came by to visit who looked exactly like Katie, down to the single dimple on her chin. I couldn't say a word; I just stood there looking at her with my mouth open. Well, she told me her brother was missing and the only clue she had is he was on his way to somewhere in the Caribbean. She was asking for my help in finding him. Strange though, the last thing she heard from him was one word—catawampus."

"He's probably on the beach somewhere. He'll turn up; trust me they always do."

"That's exactly what I told her, but I don't think so anymore. He's supposed to get married soon, and nobody has heard a word from him."

His father sniffed, "Maybe he got lost? Cold feet? Nice beaches? Could be anything, but in most cases they turn up in time, trust me." The old man looked out the window as the plane made its way out over the ocean heading for Washington. "Hmmm… you said she looked just like Katie?"

"Yeah," he said, thinking back to her. "Maybe a little bit taller, darker hair, no birthmark, but same voice and could pass as her identical twin sister. I couldn't move or say a word. She asked me to help find her him. So I told her I'd call her when I got back in town."

"So she looked a lot like Katie but not exactly?"

"Well…yeah, she really had me going. I really feel like I want to see her again. You know, just dinner or coffee or something. But you know my luck; it usually doesn't get past the second date."

"Is she married?"

"I asked, she said not anymore, whatever that means. Probably divorced, separated, or maybe even widowed. I'll find out soon enough."

"I'm sure you will. Yes, I'm sure you will. OK, you said she was part of the reason you were late, what's the other part?"

"Oh… I overslept. Sorry."

"Just what I thought. I'm taking a nap; wake me when we're close to D.C."

"Sure Pop."

Within minutes Frank Ryan was snoring as they jetted their way to the nation's capitol. Nick retrieved her card from his wallet where he put it for safekeeping. This was one business card he did not want to lose. Dr. April Kenyon, MD, he read as his hand caressed the subtle texture of her card. The soft business card felt like a silk stocking between his fingers. *Get a grip, Nick.* He did not believe in fate, but this was meant to be. It would only be forty-eight hours until he could see her again. *Wait, she said she was out of town for a few days or was it a week?* Oh well, now he had something to look forward to as the plane circled the Anacostia River making its final approach to Washington, D.C.

Chapter Eighteen

"*Life is short, and while I knew Tony Galvechio only for a little while, I was always impressed with his good heart and his willingness to help out here at Saint Matthew's,*" Father Sullivan droned on from the pulpit. "*He was well-liked and always the first to volunteer any time we needed help here at church. I remembered during our last fundraiser for our new roof, he was...*" Nick tuned him out to concentrate on his own thoughts. *He wanted to see the police file on Tony's suicide; something was nagging him. It didn't make sense, like an itch that he could not scratch.*

He also made a mental note to call the *Saint Louis Herald*. That would probably turn out to be a dead end. The young kid would show up at some beach hotel saying he wasn't going through with the wedding. Nick wanted to find out whatever he could before that happened. He looked around the nearly full church and saw Tripp Jackson, his oldest friend. Tripp was recently promoted to the Assistant Director of the FBI. Both Tripp and Tony were in his wedding; Tripp was his best man. The church was filled with well-wishers who had come to pay their respects to Tony.

As they walked outside after the service, his old friend gave him a handshake then a bear hug before shaking Nick's dad's hand.

"Good to see both of you here. How you been feeling, Frankie?"

His father took a deep breath, "Been better but what the hell, things happen when you get older, Tripp."

"I know that feeling."

"Excuse me just a minute, I see someone I need to talk with over there." Frank made his way towards a leggy blonde with dark sunglasses standing by herself who had waved at him.

"God, he never changes does he?" watching the old man hobble away wearing his most charming grin.

"No, not at all," said Nick. "Still the same old ladies' man. He still misses Mom but he's got a good one with Michelle." They watched him shake hands with his new friend and have a conversation.

"How the hell you been, Tripp?" Nick asked, with his characteristic grin.

"Good. I was shocked when I heard Tony's death. I just can't believe it."

"Neither can I. I'm going to make a couple of calls while I am in town and see if I can get in and see where it happened," Nick offered.

"Always the investigator, heh?"

"Yeah. Well some things just don't add up. I got a message from him a couple of days ago saying he was looking forward to coming to Florida next month for a fishing visit. Go figure. And what about Delgado? Did you hear anything more about Del from his station chief? "

"I made some calls right after we talked. Del was not scheduled to communicate with the office until next week. But I'm still looking into it. I was surprised he called you. He was a good man I hated to lose him."

Changing the subject Nick asked, "Tripp, you got time for a drink or dinner?"

"No, sorry, good buddy, no can do. I got my hands full. I've been working twenty-four-seven, huntin' some crazy out there. Hush-hush. You know the drill. Wish I could and wish you were back at the agency. Any chance of that happening?"

"My life is just starting to turn around. I have to let the bureau know by Christmas when my temporary leave ends. But right now, I don't think so."

"Keep it in mind. Anyone special in your life?"

"Could be. I just met a woman before I flew up here that has definite possibilities. I plan to ask her out for coffee when I get back home. She bears a striking resemblance to Katie."

Tripp's eyes narrowed then softened as he said to his oldest friend, "Hey, remember old friend, there's only one Katie. Don't try to make someone else into her. OK? Give her a chance to be her own person if you want it to go anywhere."

"Yeah, sure. You're right. But I can't wait to fly back tomorrow and see her."

Tripp glanced at his watch and said, "Gotta go. I wanted to pay my respects to Tony; he was a good guy. Take care. Stay longer next time, all right?"

"Sure. Hey, maybe come to Florida and do some fishing with the guys?"

"Rain check?"

"Sure."

"See ya."

Walking away, Nick pulled out his notepad. He knew it was old-fashioned, all of the other guys at the agency used their electronic gadgets for note taking but Nick was cut from the old school of pen and paper. He felt he could concentrate more looking at something he had written on paper.

He waved at his dad and pointed to a nearby bench. His dad waved back but turned around to talk with the tall young blonde.

"Captain Morley, please, Nick Ryan from the FBI calling," he stated when he was put through to the Montgomery County Chief of Detectives. Nick and Jedadiah "Jed" Morley went way back.

"Son of a bitch, as I live and breathe, Nick Ryan! How the hell are you? Where the hell are you?"

"I'm good, Jed, kind of. I'm in town for a funeral."
"God Nicky, sorry to hear that. Anybody I know?"

"Tony Galvechio. He was my brother-in-law."

"Aw man, damn. Christ…first Katie, now this. He was the government accountant that killed himself? Yeah, I remember that case. Anything I can do to help?"

"I'd like access to the crime scene if I could. Just to sniff around."

"Well, my guys are still checking out some leads even though it is officially classified as a suicide, so it's not really a crime scene technically, but they still have it taped off. But tell you what, I'll have a black and white meet you there and let you in. I know I don't have to say this, but if you turn up anything you'll pass it on, right?"

"Of course, Jed," business was business, and Jed didn't want to be blindsided by anything or anyone, including Nick. He didn't make captain by being somebody's fool.

Nick's next call was to *The Saint Louis Herald*, he was transferred a few times until he finally was on the phone with Matt Scott, the international editor at the paper and Sean Kenyon's boss.

"Yo, Matt Scott here."

"Matt, this is Nick Ryan. We've never spoken before but I am trying to track down a stringer that works for the Herald by the name of Sean Kenyon."

"Ryan is it?" he heard the voice say.

"Yes, sir. He's scheduled to get married in a couple of weeks and has dropped out of sight and his sister asked me to look for him."

"Yeah I know him—a young hothead. Works as a stringer and wants to do everything on his own."

Nick was beginning to get the picture of what he was dealing with, young independent journalist trying to make a name for himself.

He could hear the editor light a cigarette on the other end of the line and take a long slow draw. "I always told him to make lots of money and go buy his own newspaper and then he could do what he wanted, but until then and as long as he working for me at the *Herald* he'll do it my way. I don't think he heard me though, you know the type right?"

"Right. Have you heard from him lately? Has he checked in at all recently?"

"No, I haven't heard from him in a while. But hey, he's a stringer so I don't sign his paycheck or his expense reports since he's an independent. If he finds a good story and we publish it, we pay. But I gotta tell you... he's good. I recommended him for a permanent spot on the Metro desk. Still waiting to hear. Why do you ask?"

"Well, his sister is afraid something might've happened to him and asked me to look into it for her. So I thought I'd make a couple of phone calls and see what I could find out."

"Sorry I couldn't be more helpful, my friend. Hey listen, I gotta go, I got a newspaper to put to bed. Good to talk to you Nick."

"Thanks, Matt. Hey, one last thing. Have you ever heard Sean or anyone else use the word catawampus?"

"Hmmm...no can't say that I have," said the old-time editor. "No, that's a new one on me. I'll ask around and see if it strikes a bell with anybody here and call you if I hear anything. Sorry, Nick. Gotta go."

"Thanks, Matt. I appreciate it."

The long-time editor scribbled the words Nick Ryan and Catawampus on his yellow notepad. He circled the words for no particular reason and left his office. He had a newspaper to put out.

Chapter Nineteen

Tony Galvechio lived in the Maryland suburbs in a quiet transitional neighborhood where young couples with families were moving back, attracted by the old stately brick houses with big backyards and alleyways which lead to parking garages behind the homes. Parking was at a premium in all of the nearby neighborhoods so having a garage made the houses even more attractive.

After dropping his father off at the hotel where they were staying, Nick parked his rental car in front of Tony's home and waited for the police cruiser to show up.

A dark sedan pulled behind him and parked on the other side of the narrow one-way street. The driver shut off the engine and prepared to wait, impatiently drumming his fingers on the steering wheel. *Patience.*

Nick did not have to wait long before a police car pulled into the driveway and two uniformed officers got out. He met them at the door and followed them inside.

"Thanks for meeting me, guys."

"Hey, we didn't have much of a choice in the matter," responded the older, big one, with his tight shirt bursting from the front of his trousers. Nick let the comment pass.

"Chief said to come here and let you in, but I gotta tell you, I'm not crazy about being second-guessed by a private dick. I don't care how long you spent at the agency. But the chief is the chief, so be my guest, detective away."

"Thank you, officers."

Walking inside the familiar house brought back memories of Christmas and Thanksgiving dinners that Tony would regularly prepare for family, friends, and neighbors.

"He was found over here in the study, Agent Ryan," said the young one, Officer Church with short cropped brown hair and a small angular face.

Nick took in a deep breath. He collected himself and asked aloud to no one in particular. "He was found here, at his desk?" Nick asked.

"Yes sir, I have the photographs that were taken at the scene."

"Christ sake, Church anything else you care to share with Sherlock Holmes here?" the big one grunted. "I'm going outside for a smoke. Keep an eye on him. I don't like anyone messin' with my crime scene. And don't take forever," he said to the young officer. He walked outside without turning around, a cigarette already dangling from his lips as he searched his pockets for a light.

Nick closely examined the photos the young officer had given him and then looked at the room, the desk, and the numerous large briefcases scattered about the makeshift office and then turned his attention back to the photos.

"Officer Church, is it?"

"Yes, sir."

"According to these photos the subject was found sitting here, slumped over in his chair, with the gun on the floor under his right hand."

The young officer leaned over and looked at the photos, "Yes, sir, I presumed so, sir. You see Charlie was the investigating officer on this case along with Detective Woods, and that's probably why he is a little off today. See his signature on the report there? He's a good cop."

He read the signature on the report. "Oh yes, Officer Perciville Charles. I see why he goes by the nickname Charlie."

"What about Detective Woods? Can I talk with him?"

"Out of town on leave. His mom died. He's in Dallas and won't be back for a while. Charlie's really been the one handling this case."

"Okay, let's take a look at what we have here. The right hand held the gun, pulled the trigger and the bullet entered from here, the right side of his head, correct?

"Yes, sir."

"Hmmm, well, that can't be. You see, my brother-in-law Tony was a leftie. And if Charlie had done his homework he would've noticed it."

"Well, with all due respect Agent Ryan, Charlie, I mean Officer Charles, couldn't have known that the subject was left-handed," he stated in an effort to defend his partner.

"I don't think so, Officer Church." It was beginning to feel like a Holmes and Watson conversation, both working together. "If you look at his desk and his pen set you will see the pen on the left is out on his desk near his left hand. His phone is positioned to be answered with his left hand."

"You're right, Agent Ryan."

"Officer Church, please call me Nick. I am on leave from the agency for almost two years now. OK?"

"Sure, Nick. What else?"

"Well, take a close look at the blood splatter marks on the desk and on the floor. See anything unusual?"

The young officer peered at the photos for what seemed like an hour before saying, "No, I don't see anything out of place. What do you see?"

"Look here...close. There are blood splatter patterns on the desk and on the floor. You can see the splatter outline of what appears to be a large briefcase like the other ones over there." He pointed to the line of identical briefcases lined up by the entrance door to the office.

"Yes...?" answered the puzzled officer.

"But Officer Church, there's no briefcase. Where is it? I am sure no one moved it. My guess is it had to be taken by whoever murdered my brother-in-law and tried to make it look like a suicide."

He looked at both the crime scene and the photos again and again before saying, "You're right, Agent Ryan. CSI must have missed that. Maybe somebody else came in here looking for him and took the case from the floor?"

"Why take a briefcase? Why not money? A watch? Or other valuables? And who got in? No, I think somebody planned this and then executed my brother-in-law Tony."

"My God. I have to tell Charlie, he's the investigating officer."

"You go right ahead. But I'll put in a good word for you with Chief Morley."

"Thanks Nick. I appreciate it."

"I also suggest you double check that CSI sampled the contents of the liquor glass, and you'll probably find some type of sedative residue there."

When Nick left he found the big cop outside standing on the front sidewalk above a litter of cigarette butts. "That Officer Church is a damn good investigator; he just blew this case wide open. You better get inside and see what's going on."

"What case?" asked the befuddled cop, stomping out his cigarette on the walkway and rushing inside.

Nick drove down the quiet neighborhood street, lost in thought as to who would want to kill his brother-in-law Tony. *And why? Does this have anything at all to do with Del?* Nick didn't believe in coincidences. Not at all.

The black sedan pulled away from the curb and followed the rental car at a discreet distance before turning on its lights as it drove down the darkened street.

Chapter Twenty

Nick called Chief Morley. He was true to his word to keep the chief of detectives informed, even though the top cop got a complete rundown on the event as told by Officer Charles, who wasn't present for the findings, but still took the full credit.

Over breakfast the next day Nick shared his findings with his dad. "Tony was murdered," he said as he sipped his coffee.

His dad looked puzzled. "Why would anyone want to kill Tony?" he asked.

"Don't know. But I intend to find out." He kept reviewing his notes, photos, gun, and missing briefcase. Didn't make sense why would anyone want some old briefcase? *What was important enough inside to kill somebody for, and somebody like Tony?* "Pop, what time is our plane back to Florida?"

"Well, the flight leaves at 12:30 P.M., but I think I may stay around here for an extra day or so if you don't mind. I made a new best friend here yesterday, and she is going to show me around town for a couple of days."

"No, I don't mind, but what about Michelle? You do remember Michelle, don't you? Your girlfriend in Florida? Your roommate?"

"Oh this is nothing like that at all. Michelle and I met her in New York at the Guggenheim Museum. She's the curator of the Modern Museum of Art here, and they have some fantastic Monets in their impressionism gallery here. Private tour and all." He took a sip of coffee, "I already spoke to Michelle, and she's gonna fly up here to join me. She's also a big Monet fan. But you go on back and I'll see you in a couple days. Just be back in time for my birthday. Don't forget."

"I won't, Pop. I'll be there in plenty of time. We'll have a good time celebrating."

"My brother's coming in for it. It's a special birthday. Don't be late." He stopped for a minute before saying, "I only wish your mother were here. I still miss her so much."

"I know you do, Pop. So do I."

"I know you're anxious to meet up with your new mystery lady. Just remember what I said. What was her name again?"

"April, April Kenyon. Doctor April Kenyon. But this thing with Tony, it's nagging me. Why would anyone want him dead? He doesn't have a lot of money. He's not a ladies' man, so I can rule out the jealous husband. He doesn't gamble, so that leaves out the bookie as a suspect."

"What about at work? Did he have an argument with anyone? Or maybe he was working on something sensitive?"

"I made some phone calls and even spoke to his supervisor where he worked and he had no idea. He was well liked and working on run-of-the-mill audit stuff at DCAA. Dead-end. I'm going to snoop around here today and see if I can find out anything else."

"OK. Hey, did you find out anything about your catawampus dilemma?"

"No. I spoke to the kid's boss and he never heard him use the word and is clueless what it means. I checked it out on the internet and it just said wrong or off to the left or bogeyman. Strange. But really just another dead-end. But I still have a couple other ideas on both. I plan on speaking to his fiancée and take it from there. I am going to spend the day checking some things out. If you're going to stay in town, I'll leave you the rental car and take a cab to the airport."

"Sounds good. Let me know if I can help out at all."

"See ya later, Pop."

Dead-ends are all he found that day. He wished he would have better news when he met with April, but at least he would be seeing her again. Those big green eyes, those friendly eyes, warm eyes. He felt he was spinning his wheels as he headed to the airport to make his flight. It was not a good feeling. His phone rang as the cab pulled to the curb in front of his terminal, his caller id told him everything he needed: it was April.

"Hello? April?"

"Hi, Nick. I hope this isn't a bad time, but my travel plans were delayed, and I wanted to call you."

"Great! I'm at the airport myself, and I'll be back in Florida tonight."

"Could we do dinner tomorrow tonight? I found some notes from my brother that I wanted to show you. They may mean more to you. I couldn't make sense of them, but it did mention catawampus in them. Do you like Cuban food?"

"I love it!"

"Why don't I meet you in Delray at *Cabana Del Ray*, on Atlantic Avenue? Do you know it?"

"Sure do."

"Say seven-thirty?"

"Sure, see you tomorrow night."

Nick felt he could jump and shout at hearing her voice, and now he was going to have dinner with her! With the funeral behind him, he could focus on trying to find her brother even if he had to hike down to the islands to bring him back. Perfect! But thoughts of Tony's murder still nagged him. *Why murder some low-level government employee? Why Tony? He was such a good guy.*

He rushed to the gate rolling his only luggage behind him. The plane was loading when his phone rang again. *Maybe she wants to change the time. He could meet her tonight if she wanted.*

It was a different caller id, and he didn't recognize it or the name Weaver, only the telephone area code. The call was coming from Connecticut. "Hello?"

"Ryan? Nick Ryan?"

"Yes, this is Nick Ryan." His place in line moved closer to the agent collecting boarding passes.

"Mr. Ryan, this is James Weaver," said a refined, well-educated Ivy League voice. "I'm Vice President of Risk Management here at Century Insurance Company. I know on numerous occasions in the past you have worked with Marty Lavin in our claims investigation department."

Really. They were his biggest clients and paid most of his bills. They were his boss, but he had never spoken to anyone at Weaver's level before. It was always somebody in the claims department who contacted him. They paid well and quick. He could use the money with more work. Just not now. Please, let it not be now. Not today.

"I have a rather delicate and immediate assignment that I need you for, Mr. Ryan." The boarding line moved closer to the ticket taker.

"Yes, Mr. Weaver and what might that be?"

"One of our major clients is Universal Aircraft Maintenance Corporation. They have had two planes go down over the past two months, and now they are being deluged with lawsuits claiming they did not maintain the planes properly. The most recent crash happened a couple of days ago in Vermont. I understand you know some of the key people at NTSB."

"Yes, I went to college with the director's son Ralph Butler, and both he and his dad attended my wedding. I see them regularly but more on a social basis, but I know a lot of their field investigative people."

"I need you to get to Vermont as soon as possible and see what you can find out before the report comes out. I know that the final report will take years, but that is time I don't have, Mr. Ryan. I recognize this is short notice, but this is a crucial assignment. I need your help and expertise. We will cover all of your expenses as usual and we are prepared to double your regular fee due to the short notice involved. When can you get there, Mr. Ryan?"

His heart sank as Weaver finished talking. He took a deep breath. "I am at the Dulles airport now. I'll take the next flight and be there hopefully by later on today or tomorrow."

"Excellent, Mr. Ryan. The plane crashed near Rutland, Vermont. I'll have my secretary reserve you a room at a nearby hotel in Woodstock, Vermont. Do you have your baggage with you? Nothing checked, I presume?"

"Got everything right here with me."

"Excellent. Hold on just a minute." He was placed on hold as Nick stepped out of the line he was waiting in for his flight back to West Palm Beach. This was not going the way he had hoped.

Weaver returned to the line within minutes saying, "Since you are already at the airport, my secretary reserved a seat for you on Boston Air flight #782, gate 32, leaving in forty-five minutes. She will reserve a room for you at the Woodstock Inn, in Woodstock Vermont. I shall expect a full report as soon as you have any information at all for me. Any questions, Mr. Ryan?"

"None."

"Nick, call this number if you need anything, anything at all. Day or night. It is my private line. Thank you, Mr. Ryan. Good luck."

Nick looked up and found he was only two gates away from where he needed to be. He moved towards the gate and found his reservation just as promised, a short flight from Washington to Manchester, New Hampshire with a brief layover then on to Rutland, Vermont. He would be there well before dinnertime. He had a few minutes to spare and made the phone call he dreaded, to April.

"Hello," she said with a smiling voice big enough to be seen over the phone.

"April, hi this is Nick, Nick Ryan."

"Hi ya! I was just thinking of you. I was going to call you because I was thinking; if you're coming in today maybe we could get together tonight. If that works for you?"

"Well, that would have been great but... I have some bad news. I just had a client call me and he wants me to go to Vermont. Today."

"Oh..." she said.

"I'm sorry. I was really looking forward to getting together with you, seeing you, and... discussing your brother with you. But I got waylaid. I'll make it up to you. I promise. Oh, just to bring you up to date, I did speak with Sean's boss at the *Herald* in Saint Louis, and he said he would ask around and make some inquiries for us." *He liked the sound of that... for us.*

She was understanding, but he could tell from her voice she was disappointed. *Damn, just my luck.* He would travel to Vermont, finish his business, and hurry home as soon as he could.

"I'm staying at the Woodstock Inn in Woodstock, Vermont. Can you overnight me that information that you have about Sean. That way I can still keep busy on it."

"Sure, I can do that. And I can take a picture with my phone and send it over to your phone. Tell you what; I'll do both, how's that?"

"Great. That works." He breathed a sigh of relief; he didn't want to screw this up trying to figure out how to use his phone to find what she was going to send him.

"Thanks, Nick. I appreciate all of your help. And you know we never discussed your fee or anything. I was so upset, but I want to pay you for your time and trouble."

"We can talk about that when I see you and we see what develops. Don't worry, I'll think of something." He heard her chuckle into the phone. That was a good sign. *Hey jerk, don't even go there, she's a real lady, just like Katie. Take your time, get to know her. She may look like Katie, but she isn't, remember that. Your Katie is gone.*

The airport loudspeaker announced that his flight was boarding. "I have to go now. They are calling my flight."

"Call me... if you hear anything, Nick?" she asked, almost pleading.

"Of course. Gotta go. Talk to you soon."

Chapter Twenty-One

Nick's plane landed in Manchester, New Hampshire right on time, for a change. He grabbed his bag and made his way to the gate for his connecting flight still thinking of April. Of all the bad luck and bad timing this was the worst. He really wanted to see April, but his luck had just run out. Maybe he could make a connection with his buddies at NTSB, and they could give him a clue. God, I hope it was a pilot error, which would leave his client off the hook. *He picked up his step as he neared the deserted gate. There was no one there other than one attendant packing up getting ready to leave.*

"Hi," he said to the young twenty-something, already dreading what he was about to hear. "I am on flight #87 to Rutland. Have they boarded?"

Without looking up she said, "Cancelled. Mechanical problems. Come back later tonight, and we'll see if we can get you out on a flight then. If not, we can definitely find you a flight tomorrow." She grabbed her clipboard and began to walk away.

"Does anyone else have a flight out today?"

She stopped, turned, "To Rutland? You're kidding, right, aren't you?"

"No, I'm not. I need to get to Rutland… and soon."

She pointed to the rental car counter, "Knock yourself out. It's only a two- to three-hour drive. You'll be there in time for dinner," she said, pulling out her cell phone to answer a phone call. "It's my break time."

"How long to drive to Rutland?" he shouted.

"An hour, two…I don't really know," she said without looking back and walked away.

He loaded everything into the big SUV he rented from the agent. It was the last car available and had not even been serviced, but Nick was desperate to get to Vermont, complete his investigation, and get back to Florida. The rental agent gave him a rental agreement, a map, and directions before closing the counter and going out for a late lunch.

Once outside suburban Manchester, the traffic became sparse as he drove on the six-lane highway. The contented traveler continued to drive, the roads getting narrower and less traveled. He made his way west on Interstate I-89 from New Hampshire to the green mountains when he saw a sign, Welcome to Vermont. A while later his GPS directed him to turn off the highway onto the two-lane state road, Vermont Route #4. He crossed into Vermont and saw the mountains ahead of him. They stood there in the distance, tall and proud, like sentinels guarding the kingdom and welcoming him at the same time. Gracious soaring pine trees covered the hills and quiet valleys below.

As he drove higher into the mountains, he saw the green valleys roll by with fast-moving streams tumbling along the side of the road, their white froth displaying their own magnificence as the waters rushed by. Eager fly fishermen lined the banks casting their gentle lines behind them, arching high above their heads before being snapped back to land gently downstream. It was breathtaking. It was a scene from heaven.

Off to the right, Nick saw broad green fields stretched from the base of the majestic hills before ascending to the tall mountains shrouded in fog. It was the most beautiful countryside he had ever seen. He turned off his music to let it all soak in. His eyes devoured the scene, and he now realized why people here never left. It was beautiful. He was making good time and would soon be in Woodstock.

The valley was so green, with hardly any traffic or even houses for that matter. He opened the car window to breathe in the cool fresh mountain air and noticed a sign stating, Woodstock, 12 miles. He glanced at his watch. He would be there in time for dinner. Suddenly, the big SUV began to cough and shake. A red light on the dashboard blinked off and on before the car finally went dead. He guided the now cumbersome vehicle onto the side of the road just past a field filled with grazing horses.

Now what? he thought to himself as it began to rain. The stream by the roadside was soon filled with raging water as the mountains poured their liquid treasure down their slopes, making raging rivers from mild-mannered streams.

He tried to restart the rental. No luck. The odometer read seventy-six thousand miles on it. *Great! Just my luck.* He reached for his phone and opened the glove compartment and pulled out the rental agreement looking for the phone number. His cell phone said it all: NO SERVICE.

Damn, what was he supposed to do now? This was not his day. Now the only bright spot, April and he has to cancel his dinner with her in Florida, and then make a detour to Vermont. Then his flight was cancelled, what else could go wrong? It was then he noticed the flashing red and blue lights from the police car behind him. *Thank God, now he would get some help. See there is a cop around when you need one,* he chuckled to himself.

"Trouble with your car, sir?" An authoritative female voice asked through his open window as the rain began to let up.

"Yes…it's a rental. It just died on me, officer," he told her as he put his cell phone away not even bothering to look up.

"Could I see your license, sir?

"Yes, officer," he responded, slightly bewildered about being asked for his ID as he pulled out his wallet and drivers' license and handed it out the window. She glanced at it and handed it back to him.

"Hi ya, Nicky. Remember me?"

He looked up and saw a tall strawberry blonde standing beside the car. Sweet memories came flooding back to him. It had been a long time, a very long time.

"Megan? Oh my God! Hi ya, Meg. It's good to see you."

Chapter Twenty-Two

He looked at her standing there in front of him, her strawberry blonde hair shorter now than before, her smile just as sweet, and even the starched brown police uniform she was wearing could not hide her shapely curves. Then she smiled a flash of recognition but only for a moment. The name tag said it all, Chief of Police—Woodstock, Vermont.

"It's been a long time, Nicky, a real long time. You look good."

"You, too. How you been?" he said as he got out of the car and closed the door behind him.

"Good. What's not to like about the good life here in Vermont? Life doesn't get any better than right here. You still with the Bureau?"

"Yes, kind of… I'm still on temporary leave with them until the end of the year. What about you?"

"No," she said pointing to her chief of police badge, "I left to come here to care for my mom and never went back."

It had been six years since he had last seen her.

"You know I was surprised we never ran into one another again," he whispered.

"Well, it's been a long time. Things have changed. The last time I saw you we…"

"We were fighting and you said you never wanted to see me again, remember? I tried to call you but you didn't return my calls. I even went back to Philly and …"

"I know. It was stupid. I was stupid and… But I was so damn mad at you. Why you had to volunteer for that yearlong program in Baltimore I'll never know. And just as we were starting to…" She paused and took a deep breath.

"It was only an hour away. We could have still…"

"That's not the point. You never even discussed it with me."

The police cruiser's was flashing its red and blue patrol lights to approaching traffic. Cars whizzed by them, rubbernecking to see what the commotion was. A black sedan crawled by almost stopping before it speeded up and drove away.

"Well…?"

"Well, what?"

"What the hell ever happened to you? I never heard from you again. You went to Baltimore and I never saw you after that. What happened?"

He looked at her and saw her rising temper coming to a boil.

"I fell in love." He said it simply and directly as was his way.

"What do you mean you fell in love? I thought we were in love?"

"I thought you never wanted to see me again?"

"That's right but… You broke my … Well, if you fell in love why didn't you marry this mystery woman?"

"I did."

"What? Did you say you're married?

"Yes."

"So where is this…? Mrs. Ryan? I don't see her in your car. Huh? Where is she?"

He didn't answer her at first, reliving his pain again and again.

"Well?" she demanded.

He looked at her; the pain in his eyes told her the story. "She's dead. She was murdered almost two years ago. That's the reason I took the leave of absence, to look for her killer."

Her shoulders slumped and she gulped in air, not knowing what to say.

His eyes looked at her, begging for consolation, absolution, or just understanding. He had hidden his pain for so long, but now it was a raw and open wound.

She stumbled for words. "Oh, Nicky," she blurted out and finally pulling him close, holding him in her arms, trying to comfort him in his loss. "I am so sorry." She had opened a wound and forced him to peer into his own dark shadows. She held him close standing by the roadside. She felt his heart beating in her chest.

He looked at her standing there as it began to rain and they both were getting wet. The rain saved her as it began to pour and they made a wild dash back to her police cruiser.

They both laughed sitting in the car the rain beating on the roof. "So what brings you to my little corner of paradise?" she asked, changing the subject.

"I'm doing some investigative work for an insurance company regarding the plane that went down near here."

"Oh yes, flight #164? That's a big deal here in Vermont. How long are you here?"

"Just for a day or so max, then I head back to Delray."

"Good then, you can be my guest in town. Let me show you around. You'll love it," she said shooting him a passing glance.

His mind wandered back to their time together. Nick always thought they would get married one day, but they were sometimes like oil and water. Both of them were headstrong and hot-blooded Irish. They would have terrible fights but wonderful make-up sex. He smiled to himself thinking back to those times, some very good times.

She swallowed hard, trying to keep the conversation on track without showing her true emotions and feelings. "Is that where you are living now, Florida?"

"Yeah, I went there after Katie died to help out with my dad."

"I've missed you, Nicky."

"I've missed you too, Meg."

"Nick, I don't mean to be blunt or pry into your personal life, but…are you seeing anyone? Like on a regular basis."

He had been watching the beautiful green mountains pass by in the car windows outside as they headed west towards Woodstock.

"No, I've been dating off and on, but you know how that goes," he responded with a twinge of guilt

She stole another glance in his direction. Old feelings rose to the surface. The tall law enforcement officer turned off her flashing patrol lights and edged out into traffic.

"How's your dad? I always liked him."

"He had some back surgery recently."

"Oh? How is he?"

"He's good. Recuperating with the daily help of an overly friendly nurse, if you know what I mean."

"Yeah I do. He'll never change. Where are you staying?"

"I've got reservations at the Woodstock Inn. My client booked it for me. Is it nice?"

"Very nice. The best in town. Tell you what, let me call for a tow truck for your car and I can drop you off at the Inn and then we can both go out to the crash site."

"Sounds good. But I think I better go to the crash site first."

"OK. NTSB is still there, Mike Rogers is team leader on site."

"I know Mike. We went to Penn State then to the Academy together."

"Good. But this crash is a strange one, a very strange one."

"Why is that?"

"The scuttlebutt that I've heard around town is that it appears to be multiple systems failures, but they don't know what caused it. You know the guys come in from the site and have a couple of beers and start talking. I'm sure Mike will fill you in when we get there. Then, if you like, we can wash up and later have some dinner together. What do you think?"

He looked at her; sometimes so much in charge and other times so vulnerable, just wanting to be a good friend. "Yeah that sounds great," he responded with such enthusiasm even he was surprised at the way came out of his mouth. *What a classy lady. I remember now the things I loved about her. Bright, a good cop, a great sense of humor, sexy as hell, so full of life, so...* His mind wandered back to their time in Philly as the sun came out and began to peek from behind the clouds.

She slowed down as they drove through the quaint old town of Woodstock, Vermont, population 3,128 during the winter and over 10,000 during the fall foliage season. People stopped and waved at Megan as she drove through town.

"Hi ya, Sheriff!" was a familiar refrain. She drove through the historic, quaint Currier and Ives-like village, tucked away high in the green mountains of Vermont. The little town looked exactly what it looked like in the 1950s. It was like stepping back in time. Meg had told him she loved it here, and now Nick was beginning to see why.

"You should run for mayor."

"I have thought about it, but I just love what I do here. I would miss it."

The police car pulled off Route #4 near Bridgewater, onto a dirt road and headed to the open field crash site. Her local deputies were serving as security for the crash site warding off curious onlookers.

The car passed ten or twelve vans and television news teams trying to get pictures and camera feeds of them as they drove onto the site. Communications vans with telecommunications equipment were everywhere trying to gather information on the airplane crash in Vermont. Everybody feared terrorists and they wanted to be the first to confirm it.

She passed the crowd on the way to the site, parked the cruiser, turned off the engine, and touched his hand as he went to open the door. "Nick, before you go, I wanted to tell you I am so sorry about you losing your wife Katie. I'm sure she was a wonderful person, and I can tell she is certainly missed. My condolences."

"Thanks, kiddo," he said in a natural whisper, using the special term he called her from their time in Philly. "You would have liked her. She was very special…just like you. It took a while but they were right when they say time heals all wounds. It just takes a long time."

He turned just beyond the car, smiled, and waved at her. She grinned and returned the gesture. She had missed him and began to hum an old tune as she called her office.

Chapter Twenty-Three

Trans Global Airline flight #45 took off smoothly from New York's Kennedy Airport and headed west for fifty miles before it began its southern path to the island of Puerto Rico. Aboard the jet were 239 passengers and twelve crew members. It started as a routine flight and after meal and beverage service the evening movie was shown, one of the latest Hollywood comedies. Halfway into the movie the plane took a turbulent bump, bouncing into the air as it hit a pocket of wind shear.

Electronics Officer, Nelson Jade, checked his instrument panel and was pleased to note that nothing out of the ordinary was amiss. Just a stray pocket of wind.

"All systems go, Captain. Everything is 1020."

"Thanks for the update."

Flight Officer Jade had been with Trans Global just over a year and had decided that this was the airline for him. His regular rotation would have him flying and seeing the world. It was not like Iraq; nobody was trying to shoot him down. This is just the kind of assignment he needed after his divorce the year before from Leslie. His marriage took the stress of multiple tours in the war zone but could not take the rigors of everyday living. It had been a long drawn-out battle but he was glad it was over for both of their sakes. But in the end they had remained friends, which was rare.

A light flickered on his control panel, and then blinked before returning to normal. It blinked again. Suddenly, the plane lost all power and plunged into total darkness. Backup power brought on the lights momentarily before they too went out. The huge plane spiraled downward, out of control. Twenty-three seconds later the wing of the huge craft clipped the unmanned lighthouse before it hit the water going one hundred and fifty miles an hour. It shattered upon impact into pieces small enough to fit into a small suitcase. Sharks could be seen circling the wreckage as the debris floated to the surface. The large aviation fuel spill floating on the rough water was all that remained of TGA flight #45.

Chapter Twenty-Four

Luke Garrison sat hunched over his desk in the sub-basement of his NSA office some fourteen hundred feet below ground. He had been "promoted" to his current position of rotating "supervisor." His bosses were upset that he went over their heads and went outside the chain of command to report a strange intercept he had received. Now he could choose when and where he wanted to work as long as he kept out of their sight. This was fine with him.

The young Caltech graduate chose his work time carefully preferring when there was no one around in the buzzing computer room. The big white boxes ran themselves, and the bosses would collect the complied and distilled data reports from his desk when they came in the morning.

Working at this time of the night he could pursue his outside interest in developing applications for smart phones and test his "apps" on the NSA's powerful supercomputers. It was faster that way.

His development time on the two he had already completed was less than a week compared to the usual three months using outside computers. Luke had hoped he could sell one or two of his apps, then he and his fiancée Laura would be set for life. He figured he only had a couple of more months to work at NSA, as long as he kept a low profile and his nose clean.

He leaned closer to the bank of computer monitors in his office and checked their reporting activity. Normal and routine activity, which is just the way he liked it. He took a bite of the ham 'n' cheese sandwich his fiancée had made him before he left for work and leaned back in his chair. *Damn, it was cold in here*, he thought. *I bet they turned up the air-conditioning on these computers just to make me uncomfortable. Don't get paranoid, Luke old buddy.* That was one of the problems in working his schedule, he started talking to himself.

Luke knew they didn't like him from his first day on the job, but he didn't care. He certainly looked different from when he was recruited off the Caltech campus. They looked at him funny when he showed up at new employee orientation with his shaggy red hair and a disheveled grey and red beard. He wore army surplus khakis, a faded floral shirt, and sneakers. He knew as a supervisor he was supposed to wear a coat and tie, but it was four o'clock in the morning for Christ's sake, he thought to himself. Besides nothing ever happened here and he never saw anyone.

Not too much longer, he assured himself as he began to test the latest app he was developing. *This could be the one. Yes, this could finally be the one.* Luke began to calculate the money he would make once it was perfected and he brought it to market. He was only twenty-eight, just the right old age to sell his apps and retire to some tropical island paradise. His mind drifted to how he and Laura would spend their time in Hawaii, on the beach, drinking colorful rum martinis from a coconut.

The young techie heard the faint sound of a short warning beep coming from one of the computers. He swung his chair around and walked down between the rows and rows of the huge white computers. Everything was white in this room, the floor, the computer hardware, the desks, the clocks, everything but Luke, who was wearing his favorite flowered Hawaiian shirt.

Luke heard the brief noise again and hurried to the offending hardware. It was droning on as it was supposed to, but the beeping noise it had made intrigued Luke. He set down his illegal smart-phone and moved a chair in front of the control panel on computer number #849. It was doing everything it was supposed to be doing. *Maybe it was his imagination? Yes? That's what it was.*

He stood and started to walk away but thought better of it and quickly sat back down and took control of the system. He stopped for a moment to assess his situation. *Remember, this is how you made enemies before, Luke. Remember? Are you sure you want to do this?* He took a deep breath and ignored the little voice inside him. He pressed on.

The computer was his now, his to command.

He typed in: COMPUTER-SWITCH TO VOICE COMMANDS. The computers whirled and hummed electronically in response.

"Sara, I need you to run a background check for me."

"Hi Luke. I've missed you," his computer said in a female voice which sounded remarkably like his fiancée's.

"Hi Sara. I need you to list activity—last four minutes," he muttered his audible instructions. He switched over to an unnamed male voice. He was not doing algorithms any longer, he now meant business.

In the blink of an eye, it began to update him on the screen of its past activity over the last two hundred and forty seconds—four billion instances and still counting. He forgot who he was dealing with, but he was the boss. He just had to speak their language.

"COMPUTER, STOP. COMPUTER, LIST ABNORMAL ACTIVITY—IN LAST FIVE MINUTES." He could hear the systems beginning to whirl, their drives and intelligence collecting and collating the response he needed.

"One billion and counting." No damn computer was going to get the best of him.

"COMPUTER, STOP." He needed to try a different tact. "COMPUTER, WHAT DOES AN AUDIBLE ALERT SIGNIFY?"

"Enormous digital data activity. An anomaly."

"COMPUTER, DEFINE ENORMOUS."

"DDB."

"COMPUTER, WHAT IS A DDB? PLEASE ANALYZE AND REPORT."

"Digital Data Blast bytes of centillium bytes per second. It is a data signal request capable of overwhelming any data system." *How much is that,* he wondered, having never heard the figure before that day? *Damn, what have I started?*

"COMPUTER, HOW MUCH IS A CENTILLIUM?"

"One thousand quinquagintillion."

What the hell does that mean? "COMPUTER…NEVER MIND."

He stood up and sat down. Nervous. "COMPUTER…LIST OCCURRENCES OF DDB IN…SAY THE LAST YEAR. ALL OCCURRENCES, COMPUTER."

The computer's job was done in seconds. "Six."

"THANK YOU, COMPUTER. COMPUTER, PRINT DATA SHEET ON ALL DDB ACTIONS. DATE, TIME, DURATION, AND STRENGTH."

He read through the computer printout, trying to find a pattern, some rhyme or reason to it. There was no rationale to the numbers other that it happened first in a short burst, then a long one.

He stopped, "COMPUTER, WHY IS THERE A SHORT BURST OF DATA, AND THEN A LONG BURST?"

"First burst is a quantum handshake. The second is the DDB."

"WHAT IS A QUANTUM HANDSHAKE?" Silence.

"COMPUTER, WHAT IS A QUANTUM HANDSHAKE?"

"It is what is used as an electronic identifier."

"COMPUTER, WHAT DO YOU MEAN AN IDENTIFIER?"

"It assures that the data acquisition target is correct."

"Hmmm. COMPUTER, ONE LAST THING. WHAT IS A DDB ANOMALY?"

"A powerful weapon. Sir, this information is now classified a Level Six priority report."

A chill went through his whole body, causing him to shake at what he had just heard. He swallowed hard because he had only had one Level Six Priority Report the whole time he had worked at the Agency. The last time it nearly cost him his job but instead the government gave him a promotion. *Go figure. Damn, why didn't he just mind his own business?*

"COMPUTER, WHAT DOES A DDB DO?"

"It overwhelms then annihilates its target with digital data causing the targeted system to malfunction and shut down."

"COMPUTER, LIST THE TARGETS FOR THESE DDBS. AND REPORT WHERE THESE DDBS EMANATED FROM." He heard the pulsating whirling noise again for a brief second.

"No data currently available. Classified Level Six—Priority"

"COMPUTER, CHECK TO SEE..." He changed his mind and sat down in front of the monitor and took command of the keyboard. The young techie furiously began to type instructions and queries to the computer. He sometimes liked the old-fashioned way of handling the computer.

Months ago he had placed a standing instruction that he be notified if any anomalies were ever found. *Why didn't that happen?* Scrolling through his entries, he found out why. Someone had overridden it! Who the hell would do that, and why was somebody countermanding his orders? He searched further. Why would someone do that? He continued to search until he found the justification entry that JDB would have been required to post. His boss. There it was— Alert loud and too annoying. Stop all alerts."

"Computer, monitor and report all future DDBs only to my station location directly. No audible alert. Thank you, computer. Computer, also, please print report of the DDBs discovered and mark it a Level Six Communications—DIO (Director of Intelligence Operations)—Eyes Only. Good night, computer, and take the rest of the night off."

He chuckled to himself, joking with the multibillion-dollar computer hardware.

"Good night, sir. And sir, the final answer on the application you are developing. Answer is: Twelve to the tenth power will deliver you your desired result on your new application. All numbers will then be sequenced."

Luke Garrison was no longer paying attention to the computer; he had bigger problems he had to address. And he needed to do it now. It was seven A.M., and somebody had to be on the top floor by now; this time he was going to follow protocol. He searched through the thick binder of protocol instructions for Section Five and searched through the protocol list until he found what he was looking for *Level Six Communications—Contact the Office of the Director Immediately.* He reread the protocol instructions. *Shit! Not again.*

Luke picked up the phone, and dialed the director's office. "This is Luke Garrison, International Data Supervisor, Section Five. I have a Level Six Priority Protocol Directive that I need to share with the director or executive duty officer."

The duty agent responded immediately, "Bring it to the director now."

The word sounded strange, DDB. It gave him the chills as to its potential to do harm. Computers were supposed to help people; they were supposed to make life easier. Not this time, he thought, as he headed for the elevator and for his meeting with the new director. No computer anywhere would be safe.

Chapter Twenty-Five

Luke felt ill at ease in his hastily retrieved purple tie that had been languishing in his desk drawer for months. It hung around his neck and was securely fastened below his Adam's apple, lying against his bright yellow floral Hawaiian shirt. Some first impression he was going to make with senior management. Who cares? *He had bigger problems on his mind.* Who was using this newfound weapon and against whom? With the blasting of a computer command it could disable any computer, anywhere—turn off an electrical grid, sabotage a city's power supply, shut down a bank, an elevator, open prison cells, down an airplane, anything and cause catastrophic damage. And why? To what end? *No answers, just a lot of questions.*

The elevator opened on the executive floor, and he was immediately greeted by two large men in dark suits and dark ties.

"Yes...?" asked the big one.

"I'm Garrison, Luke Garrison. I called earlier, and they told me—" The taller one did not let him finish and instead walked away as he spoke into his sleeve after perusing Luke's identity badge while the big one placed his large hand against Luke's chest.

"Please wait here, sir," he said without taking his eyes off Luke even for a moment. The three of them stood in the lobby of the executive offices in an awkward silence waiting for James Holmes, the new Director of Intelligence Operations at NSA.

Luke had only seen Holmes's picture on the wall of the cafeteria as he went through the line during his frequent trips there. Photos of every director since its inception in 1952 were hung on the wall for all to see. The cafeteria was open twenty-four hours a day because the work at NSA never looked at the clock. *Vigilance Never Sleeps* said the motto over the front door as you entered the main building and was repeated on the red plush carpeting beneath his feet. He moved his feet to create waves of ripples in the soft wool rug. *Feels good, must be wool.*

He would love to take off his shoes and feel if the carpet was as plush as it seemed beneath his shoes or maybe he would just touch it with his hand. He looked up to see the glare from his two guards and thought better of it.

A short stocky man with no chin and very little hair approached the three men. He stuck out his hand, but when Luke went to shake it the director said, "Let's see your Level Six report." Luke handed him the red and white folder with the large Roman numeral six stamped on the outside.

As the director became engrossed in reading the report he commented out loud without looking up, "No need to get all dressed up to meet with me Mr. Garrison. I'm only the top dog here."

Before he could respond Holmes spun around and barked at his security detail, "Get the car, we are going to see Jackson at Cyber Command. Garrison, you come with me. I want you in this meeting. If what you say is true this is something that we have always feared could happen and now…" his voice trailed off.

"Yes, sir," said Luke smartly.

The retired general stopped and peered over his round tortoise-shell glasses and eyeballed the young man standing before him. "Let's go!" he commanded the group.

Chapter Twenty-Six

The three men settled into the back seat of the big limousine and moved quickly to cover the short distance to the headquarters building of the United States Cyber Command some three blocks away.

While the NSA command center building was towering and intimidating, the Cyber Command office, was just two stories. It appeared as just another one of the many tan and grey office buildings that littered the suburban landscape in and around the nation's capitol in Southern Maryland. The car rolled out quietly from the underground garage towards its destination picking up speed.

"Listen up, Garrison," said Holmes. "Protocol now requires us to show any data threats, Level Five and above to those cowboys at Cyber Command. I don't like it and never have, but they'll learn that the gravy train doesn't always run on time. I'm required to bring you since you are the author of this report. So, just stand there, nod your head if you're asked a question, but whatever you do, don't open your mouth. Do you understand me?"

"Yes, Mr. Director."

"OK, we're almost there, just remember what I told you. Lips zipped. Got it?"

"Yes, sir."

"Oh, and by the way, where on earth did you get that tie?"

"My girlfriend bought it for me for my birthday, sir," he said with a smile.

"It's atrocious looking." The director looked to the security guard who accompanied them on their trip and just rolled his eyes.

"Showtime," he said as the car pulled to a stop in front of a small nondescript office building. It was still within sight of the NSA building they had just left.

They paused to show their ID badges to the waiting security officials, when a tall distinguished-looking man, with sharply chiseled facial features and short cropped hair, marine style, walked from a nearby elevator. He sported a bushy, unkempt handlebar mustache, wearing a tan suit coat, white shirt, and... a bright purple tie. It was identical to Luke's tie.

"Good morning, Director Holmes. Follow me, sir. I'm Matt Rowe, Deputy Director of United States Cyber Command. Director Jackson is expecting you. We will join him in the executive conference room." They pinned on their visitor badges and watched the elevator door close behind them. He turned to Luke, "You must be Garrison."

"Yes, sir," Luke said with a smile as Rowe shook his hand.

"I've been hearing good things about you and your work Luke."

"Thank you, sir. I try."

"Well, keep it up. We need good people like you in our line of work," he said with a grin before turning to a red-faced Holmes. "Careful Jimmy, we may try to steal your star here if you're not careful." Rowe lean close and whispered, "Nice tie. Birthday gift?"

"Yes sir, from my fiancée."

The elevator doors opened, and they were greeted by a tall shapely, well dressed woman with short black hair pulled back behind her ears. She smiled and motioned them down the hallway.

"Good morning, gentlemen, the director is waiting for you in the conference room. Please follow me."

The glass meeting room at the end of the lush green-carpeted passage had a long cherry conference table with row upon row of black and chrome leather chairs beside it. A picture of the current president adorned one wall at the end of the long table and a large Andy Warhol original print hung on the other wall.

Jack Jackson, the director of the America's newest agency, was a forgettable sort of man, of average height, average weight, thinning hair but eyes that went from inquisitive and kind to piercing and dark. He turned those keen eyes on Luke, who felt them studying his every move as he walked to his chair and sat down. The stare burrowed through him like a hot blowtorch until the Director was satisfied with his evaluation. Luke saw the computer mind spinning and whirling as it processed the information it had retrieved on him. The young techie dared not look away. Finally, Jackson was done his examination and spoke in a slow but measured voice.

"How did you come across this information, Mr. Garrison?" he asked, coming directly to the point, asking now with inquisitive eyes while ignoring everyone else in the room.

Luke wanted to answer this man in the same manner as the question was asked, direct and to the point but remembering what his boss had said in the car earlier.

"I… I," he stammered. He swallowed, *the hell with it*, he thought, "I responded to a Signal Alert on my monitoring computer, sir. It's one I had set it up a few months ago."

"And then the computers told you all of this?"

"No sir, not at first. So I just kept asking questions until I got the answers I wanted."

The director laughed and suddenly became animated as he looked around the room before saying, "Damn, now that's what I like to hear. Somebody showing some goddamn initiative around here and has some curiosity. You need to come to work for us, Luke," he proffered with his imploring eyes.

Holmes coughed and interrupted, "Well, Jack, he has been with us for over seven years and has a shining career path with our agency. Besides we're all on the same team. Right?" interjected his now fuming boss.

Jackson ignored him, his gaze still locked on Luke. "What do you make of this report Luke?"

"I don't know yet at this point, Mr. Director. But I don't like it. I plan to continue to monitor the activity and see if I can find out what the hell is going on, sir."

"Good. Copy me directly on any further activity you may find. I mean anything and everything. Do you understand me, son?"

"Yes, sir."

"We have to put a stop to whoever is doing this before they start shutting down computers everywhere. People will die. Luke, do you have any idea where this DDB came from? Or what the target was or if it connected?"

"No, sir, I don't. I'm still working on it. But it appears to be coming from two separate locations. The quantum handshake is coming from one location, and the DDB is coming from somewhere else."

"Stay on it, Luke. I'm going to assign a liaison and a team of analysts to work with you to see what else we can find out. Thank you, gentlemen, for coming here today and bringing this information to my attention." He smiled and continued, "Luke, I'm going to ask Matt, my second in command, to give you the cook's tour of our little workshop here while I have a private conversation with your director for a few minutes. Very nice to meet you, Luke," he said and rose to shake his hand. "Think about what I said today. Good to meet you."

Luke's mind was still spinning from all the wonderful things he had seen during his tour when he returned to cubicle office. His shift was over, and it was time to go home. He was tired and grabbed his car keys and his knapsack from the floor. *Way to keep your mouth shut, dummy. Time to go home and get some sleep. It's been a long day.* It was then he noticed an alert on his computer screen flashing:

DANGER! DANGER!
DDB Incidence Alert!
DDB activity—handshake 8:30 A.M. Zulu time

Chapter Twenty-Seven

Nick Ryan walked past the crash site toward a long table and a group of men milling about it when he heard a familiar voice shout, "Son of a gun! Will you lookie here! Nick Ryan!" Mike Rogers stammered in amazement. "I'll be damned, I can't believe it's you and after all this time. Where the hell you been all these years, Nicky? Damn, it's good to see you."

"I took a leave of absence when Katie was killed."

"Oh my god, that's right. I was in Australia when I heard. I couldn't believe it, Katie gone. You have my sympathies, Nick. He turned to his old friend and asked, "Want some coffee?"

"Yeah, I'd love some."

"Follow me," he said as they walked inside the huge tent with tables all around the perimeter filled with computers, files and airplane parts. In the center of the tent were the charred remains of the reconstructed airplane.

"Wow, this is some operation!"

"It is. This is one of the most dedicated and effective organizations I've ever worked for, including the agency. Which brings me to the question, what brings you this neck of the woods?" he asked, his arm draped on Nick's shoulder.

"I'm doing some investigative work for Century Insurance. They insure the maintenance company, and they were a little nervous when the plane went down. They asked me to look into it and see what I could find out."

"Well, even though you shouldn't be here …. You know we only allow NTSB investigators near the crash site and here in the tent. But let me show you how we operate. Just keep a low profile, OK?"

"Sure."

"We have separate teams who report to team leaders who look into twelve different areas relating to the crash. I'm the onsite commander and all of the team leaders report to me. We first look at the plane, the weather, the operations, aircraft maintenance, aircraft manufacturers and recalls. We then look at the electrical, weather instrumentation, power plants, human performance, air traffic control, airport guidance, survival factors, witnesses, and of course the FDR and CVR."

"What are FDR and CVR?"

"That stands for flight data recorder and the cockpit voice recorder."

"Gotcha, then what?"

"Once we have all of this, we put together a preliminary report and issue a statement."

"What do you think happened?"

"Officially, it is too early to tell. But I think this was deliberate. I just don't know yet by whom or what. But I will, give me time."

"I believe you. Off the record, could the cause have anything to do with maintenance?"

"Ask me that on Tuesday?"

"Why then?"

"Well, the plane left Rutland Airport and made a routine flight to Boston then fueled up and returned here to Vermont. We have a videotape of the night watchman near the plane before it left here for Boston. It looks kind of suspicious. He was a former mechanic for the airline, now on disability and had just been told he was going to be laid off, so… draw your own conclusions. Revenge? Payback? Who knows? I can tell you there was a massive systems failure."

"Interesting. So you think he may be the missing link?"

"We'll know in two to three days. He's in Canada somewhere camping and hunting out in the boonies and is scheduled to be back between now and Tuesday, just a few days. We got the RCMP, the Mounties and everybody else looking for him. But Nick, I can't tell you anything more, you understand? I'm not supposed to say even that to anyone outside the Board."

"I appreciate it Mike. Anything else that I should know?"

The tall red-haired investigator leaned close to his old friend and whispered, "There are some agency guys, nobody I know, and also a bunch of suits hangin' around here with full clearance. Don't know who they are with but they carry some heavy muscle, if you know what I mean?"

"Hmmm. OK, thanks, Mike. I'll check back in with you on Tuesday if that's no problem."

"Sure, I'll be here. Twenty-four-seven as they say, as usual."

"Hey, what's the guy's name that's in Canada?"

"Last name is Stugen, Willie Stugen. Good seeing you again, Nick. Maybe we can do dinner in town one night?"

"I'm staying at the Woodstock Inn."

He began walking back to the car and pulled out his cell phone to see if he had service. He had three missed calls but no messages. One call originated in Florida, was from his dad, one from Century insurance, and one was from area code 314. He called his dad.

"Hello?"

"Hey Pop, how ya doin'?"

"Hiya. I'm good. Where the hell are you?"

"Vermont."

"Vermont? What the hell are you doin' in Vermont?"

"Got a call from a client and had to make a detour to Vermont. They asked me to look into a recent plane crash here."

"Well, my plans changed as well. Michelle was not feeling well so I'm back in Florida."

"Nothing serious, I hope?"

"Naw, I think she was just missing me and wanted to go home."

"You do have that effect on some people, Pop."

His father lowered his voice and used a tone of voice that Nick immediately recognized, something was serious. "Nicky, I went by your place to drop some stuff off, and one of your neighbors said there were a couple of guys in suits asking all kinds of questions about you. They wanted to know where they could find you."

"Who were they?"

"She didn't know, and they didn't leave a card or anything. You know Delores and how she gets. It may be nothing, maybe just musings of an old flirt or ... Just watch your back. OK, son?"

"Sure, Pop. I'm going to be here for a little while then I'll be heading home. Oh, before I forget, I ran into an old friend, Megan Carter."

"Megan? What's she doing in Vermont?"

"She is the chief of police here in the town of Woodstock."

"I always liked her. I always thought you would wind up with her one day. Now don't get me wrong, I loved Katie like one of my own, but that Megan was something special. Give her a kiss for me, OK?"

"Sure, gotta go."

"Be careful, Nicky. Love ya."

"Love ya too, Pop."

Nick called his client. Weaver answered on the first ring. "This is Weaver. Ryan?"

"Yes, sir. I was just on site. Spoke with the site commander, a Mr. Michael Rogers, who I used to work with years ago. He said it was still way too early in the investigation to make any determination, but he told me they are looking into a person of interest." Nick paused to let the information sink in.

"Go on Ryan, you have my attention."

"Well, I can't say anything more at this point other than this person is out of the country for a few days but is expected back at any time over the next few days. He was seen near the aircraft before it took off. What would you like me to do?"

"Stay there until he returns and keep me informed. Good work, Ryan." The phone went dead. *Pleasant way to end a phone conversation.*

He dialed the next number, a 314 area code, it rang four times before someone answered, "*Saint Louis Herald*, International Desk, Matt Scott here."

"Matt? Hi, it's Nick Ryan. I saw you tried to reach me, but there was no message. Must be something with this mountain air or something, so I thought I would…"

"Nick, tell me more about this catawampus thing?" he asked, straightforward. "Where did it come from? And what do you think it means? And what's your connection to it?"

"Like I mentioned on the phone, Sean Kenyon's sister April asked me to look into why she hasn't heard from him for a couple of weeks, and the last text message she got from him just said one word, catawampus, that's all. Why do you ask? Did you find out anything?" The mention of April's name sent a warm quiver down his spine.

"Wait, let me close my office door."

Nick waited as he heard the editor walk and heard a door slam shut in the background.

"I made a couple of phone calls for a story we were working on and I happened to ask my source if the word catawampus meant anything at all to him. The next thing I know I got two big goons in dark suits, white shirts, and black ties crawling up my butt askin' all kinds of questions. I told them what I knew, and they stayed for awhile asking me questions before they left."

"Who were they?" he was puzzled over these recent events, first his mysterious visitors in Florida now this. *What the hell is going on?*

"Don't know. I was hoping you could tell me. Keep your ears open and stay in touch, Nick."

Can't be government guys, they always leave cards. The mob? What on earth would they want with me? He reached the car and saw Megan finishing her phone call. She was the only bright side to staying here, but he felt torn. He had known Megan for years, but with April she was his Katie. *God, how much more screwed-up can this get?*

"Well, it looks like you're stuck with me for awhile. I'll be here for a day or so. They're waiting for some fisherman to come back from his camping trip somewhere in the boonies of Canada. They are looking for someone by the name of Willie Stugen."

"I know Willie. Nick, I would be pleased to have you here for as long as you want to stay."

"Well, they think he has some valuable info that could help their investigation."

"Nick, before we go back to town I want to show you something, one of my favorite places," she said pointing to the hillside above the town.

The drive to Mount Eden took thirty minutes and the hike to the summit took another fifteen minutes. When they reached the peak it provided a panoramic view of the Vermont countryside for miles and miles around. Nick felt that from where he was sitting he was witnessing something magical.

"This is my most favorite place in the world," said Meg in a reverent whisper as she sat down on an old wooden bench. "You can see the mountains in the distance, the green valleys below and the rivers and the falls meandering down the mountainside."

"I see why you love this place so much." He put his arm around her. They sat for awhile without saying a word, as if in church paying homage to God's wonderful creation that spread out before them. They looked out over the dark green valley below filled with bristly pine trees, tall oaks, and majestic chestnut trees spread below them and saw Lake Woodstock in the far distance.

They walked down the mountain path hand in hand both lost in thought about the future. Where would the next couple of days lead? Time was growing short for both of them, and they both realized it. Life was full of mysteries, but fortune had smiled on her. She now had more time with him. She dropped him off at the hotel and said, "I'll pick you up, say eight o'clock?"

"Perfect," he said with a smile. "See you tonight."

Chapter Twenty-Eight

Matt Scott felt like a cub reporter again as he sifted through all the information and notes he could find about what the young kid Kenyon was working on. He was first upset with Ryan for calling him and breaking his concentration and causing him to lose focus while trying to publish the paper. Now he thought he was onto something. Catawampus? What the hell did it mean?

He had to admit that it made him feel young again, like when he first started in the newspaper business. He would call Ryan just before the edition hit the streets as he promised and give him an update. He was proud of his work putting the pieces together. All he needed was to verify some leads and *The Saint Louis Herald* would be on top once again, being the first on the street with the scoop. The seasoned editor clicked his heels like a silly school kid. *What a story!*

Looking at his watch, he saw it was two-thirty A.M. and the usually bustling newsroom was now deserted. He grabbed the folder with the draft of his story and headed for the walkway that led to the garage. His car was parked on the tenth floor, corner spot with his name stenciled on the curb. They gave him his own parking spot rather than a raise, which was fine with him. He would have worked for free at the *Herald* he loved it so much.

There was only one other car in the garage. He didn't mind working late, never did. It was easier now since Martha left him, no one to nag him about his drinking and his long hours. Probably for the best, he thought as he sat in his car and turned on the ignition. It was then he saw it, a folded twenty dollar bill under his windshield wiper. He squinted not believing his eyes and turned off the engine and opened the car door to reach for the money. He had to leave the car to pull it from under the wiper and sure enough, it was a crisp new twenty-dollar bill. Holding the money he snapped it between his hands. *My lucky day!*

When he looked up he saw the big man moving towards him, his hands outstretched. He instinctively walked backwards, but the man kept coming towards him. The words didn't leave his lips as he went back further and further. It was all happening so quickly. His back bumped up again the outside wall of the building. There was nowhere else to go. He looked behind him then back at the silent interloper.

Chino pushed his chest with both hands and watched the longtime editor tumble into the air, his head bouncing off the wall. He landed with a loud thump some ten floors below. The editor's body twitched once but then he was gone.

He grabbed the folder from the front seat of the dead man's car and climbed into the sedan parked next to it. The disabled surveillance camera lay on the floor of the front seat of his rental and the big man drove away. His job was done.

Chapter Twenty-Nine

The Woodstock Inn was a large white New England mansion-like hotel with a broad expanse of lush green lawn serving as its front yard with a line of tall oak trees which shielded it from view from the street. It was on South Park Street on the Green, and not far from the center of town and the town square. It was a combination of New England elegance and Southern hospitality.

A uniformed doorman, wearing a top hat and a green velour jacket greeted Nick as he swung the large glass front door open for him. "Welcome to the Woodstock Inn and Resort. Enjoy your stay, sir." Another immediately took his bag and followed him inside.

Once indoors walking on the dark-stained oak floor, he could not help but notice a huge fireplace in the lobby area. It was well over four feet tall and at least eight feet wide. A hand carved wooden bench sat in front of the massive structure. The fresh smell of pine filled the air along with the chatter of guests with tennis racquets making their way outside to the tennis courts.

He could see a bar off to the right and the restaurant straight ahead. The place was busy, very busy but nobody seemed rushed. Nick noticed every employee who walked by greeted him with a smile. It had a warm, comfortable New England feel to it.

After he checked in, he was shown to his room by a bellhop who rambled on about all of the activities available for visitors, but he wasn't listening. He was still thinking about April, the men searching for him, and about his evening with Megan. *This was getting complicated.* He showered, shaved, and changed clothes. Meg said it was casual, and he was done just in time to grab the elevator and head downstairs to the lobby.

Megan drove her Range Rover under the front portico promptly at eight o'clock and handed the keys to the doorman. She stood outside the car as Nick walked down the broad entryway steps towards her.

"Hi ya," she said with a smile. "I wasn't sure if you'd be ready. Your car is over there. Something to do with the fuel line being clogged," she said pointing to his rental car parked off to the side in a nearby reserved spot in front of the hotel.

Nick was not really paying attention. He could not take his eyes off of her. She was gorgeous. Her uniform had hidden many of her most wonderful assets.

Megan was now dressed in a tan, sheer silk blouse with form-fitting white slacks which showed off her curvaceous figure and matching white sandals. She looked more like the college model she used to be than a cop. Around her neck was a white and gold blister pearl necklace. She touched it fondly when she noticed Nick looking at it.

"Remember this, Nicky? You gave it to me on our one-year anniversary."

"I remember it well. I also remember how we celebrated that night."

She blushed, which was unusual for her.

"Sorry," he quickly commented not wishing to embarrass her.

"Don't be. Come on let's eat, I'm famished" she said smiling, changing the subject. Nick liked a woman who wasn't afraid to show her true feelings.

"Do you mind walking? It's not far. It's such a beautiful night, like most nights in Vermont."

"Not at all. Was that another sales plug for Vermont that I just heard?" he asked.

"Kind of," she laughed.

He wanted to hold her hand as they walked but also knew that she lived in this small town and as sheriff held a very responsible position there. He was familiar with small towns and the destructive nature of gossip.

They walked a block, and she smiled then stretched out her hand for his; their hands fit together perfectly. Her hand felt warm as it melded into his. She leaned close and whispered, "It's a small town, but they mind their own business here in Vermont. Besides they probably already think we are sleeping together," she said with a laugh. He took in a deep breath and squeezed her hand. They passed the old covered wooden bridge on Mountain Avenue. It was like living in a Norman Rockwell kind of town.

"I made reservations for us at Claire's. It's right on Central off the town square just a few minutes away. A little quirky, but I think you'll love it."

The New England hotspot was full and the waiting crowd was overflowing out into the street. The old historic building, with its saloon entrance doors, squeaky dark oak floors and an old bar, which greeted visitors as soon as they walked inside was the perfect place for them to spend the evening. The main dining room was off to the left with other tables staggered past the bar on the right. Narrow stairs to the second level were behind the bar. In the back a DJ was playing dinner music at the rear of the restaurant around a small dance floor.

"Here we are my friends," the young waiter said sitting them near the back at the upper level overlooking a small center area with about six tables. He laid the menus on the table and said with somber voice, "Enjoy it while you can."

"Why? What do you mean? You're not closing are you?" Meg asked.

"Maybe. The owners are looking to retire. Hope I have a job at Christmas."

They ordered dinner and some wine, "Just one glass," she said, "I'm drivin' remember?" She smiled at him while pretending to look over the menu.

"I meant to ask you, how's your mom doing?"

She took a deep breath then looked up, "She died two years ago. I'm glad I did what I did coming up here to care for her and my Aunt Helen, but it was the toughest time in my life. I had to watch her suffer and die a little more each day. The end was almost a welcome relief."

"Meg, I'm so sorry to hear that. I really liked your mom and your aunt. My condolences," he reached for her hand to comfort her.

They talked and talked. The words came pouring out of both of them trying to catch up and learn everything that had happened in their lives. Their hands brushed against one another once when reaching for the bread on the table, and Nick felt his old feeling for her stir. He listened to her and looked into her eyes; he was lost and now he knew it. When the conversation paused, Nick finally asked her, "You never married?"

"No, I came close, but it just never worked out I guess." *He's the same sweet man I always knew. He's kind, considerate, and so easy on the eyes. I will never forget the flowers he sent my mother on her special birthday. What happened to the two of us? It just wasn't meant to be. It doesn't matter now. I have three days, only three days.*

The dinner crowd was thinning out and a younger group began to take over the nearby tables. Two of the newest arrivals nearest them, both the size of football players, became boisterous and began shoving one another.

"Excuse me for just a minute," she told him and walked over to the two offending brutes, who towered over her.

Nick started to join her, but she waved him away. He stood ready to help, just in case she needed it.

She grabbed each by the neck and brought them into her own huddle. She showed them her badge and whispered something he couldn't hear. They looked at her, sizing her up before shaking her hand and then sat down.

"What did you say to them?"

"I told them I had a hot date tonight and if they kept it up they were going to spend time in jail, and it would be time they would always regret. That's all. Come on, let's dance," she said grabbing his hand.

"Sure, Sheriff," he said smiling. A DJ playing soft dinner music announced, "Ladies and gentlemen this is the last song of the night. Grab a partner and have a dance."

As they danced he held her in his arms and pulled her close. He could feel her warm breasts beating against his chest. The tenderness of her body pressing against him brought back even more memories as they continued to dance. It was as if they had never been apart. He kissed her neck and held her closer. It was getting late.

"Want to come back to my place for a drink? Say a glass of champagne?" she asked in a whisper.

"Wonderful. I was thinking the same thing."

In the darkened parking lot, he put his arms around her neck and kissed her. "That's from my dad. He said to give you a kiss when I saw you."

She pulled him close and kissed him a long lingering, smoldering kiss, a kiss he had been waiting forever since he first saw her. It seemed to last forever. He kissed her, and their bodies melded. He could feel her heartbeat and her breasts heave against his chest. Her warmth melted him, and he wanted her more than ever. The next kiss never seemed to end, his hand slid underneath her blouse, searching, searching…

Her hand traveled down his chest, to his stomach, and continued lower.

"Time to go," she said in a voice hoarse with passion. "Come on, I don't live far, just off the main drag in West Woodstock. It won't take long to get there, I promise."

"Or we can order room service at the hotel?"

"That is probably not a good idea, small town and all."

"Right." He looked across the street, the pharmacy was closed. "I need to stop at the hotel, just for minute? I just need to get…something…from my room. It'll only take a minute."

"Nick, tell you what. I'll drop you off there. Then give you directions to my place. That will give me some time to straighten up at my place and ice down the champagne and change into something…more comfortable. It's real easy to find, just off the main road, Route #4 and make a right onto Prosper Road. OK?"

"Sure, that works."

She jotted down the simple directions and kissed him again before driving away. He could still taste her lipstick and smell the lingering scent from her floral perfume as he went inside the hotel.

Nick ran to his room from the elevator and began a furtive search of his toiletry bag until he finally dumped the contents on the bed. He found what he was looking for, shoved them into his pocket, and headed for the door. When it swung wide open, standing before him were two large men in dark suits and dark ties. "Nick Ryan? We've been looking for you. Please come with us."

Chapter Thirty

"Excuse me? Who the hell are you?"

The tall one, without breaking a stride, ignored Nick and reached for his arm. "You will need to come with us...now"

"Not without an ID and some explanation of what this is all about."

The older one, reached inside his jacket and pulled out his government credentials, "We're with the Anti-Terrorist Task Force (ATTF) and you're wanted for questioning regarding the downing of the airplane outside of Rutland, among others." They each flashed an ATTF badge with a picture ID. He briefly saw the last name on one the big one showed him. He was called Robson.

Maybe he could charm his way out of this. "Well, gentlemen, can't this wait until tomorrow? I was on my way to an important meeting with a very lovely lady, one that I really do not want to miss, if you know what I mean."

"This is a matter of national security, and I'm afraid that we must insist you come with us Mr. Ryan." Ryan could tell he had no sense of humor.

"Well, can I at least call her and tell her I will be detained?"

"No, you can do that later Mr. Ryan. For now we need to clear some things up."

"Clear what up?"

"Catawampus, Mr. Ryan. Now let's go."

Catawampus? I'm beginning to hate that word. "I don't know anything about it. It's just a word somebody used."

They began to walk away with Nick firmly in tow.

"Am I under arrest?"

"No, you are being brought in for questioning for a case we are working on."

"I'm with the FBI, on temporary leave. Let me show you my ID."

The two special agents slowed down for a minute and looked at him. The taller one finally grunted, "Later Ryan." They walked down the rear stairs and Nick sat in the rear of the car. Robson drove the dark sedan away, heading out of town.

They headed West on SR#4, passing the crash site with its growing legion of TV vans, and cars filled with reporters. It was then Nick saw a sign that said West Woodstock and then saw the turnoff for Prosper Road where Megan lived. He was sure Meg was waiting for him and probably wondering what was taking him so long. He thought about Megan and his current predicament. He would get this cleared up once he talked to someone in authority. His mind wandered.

What the hell is this all about? I don't even know what catawampus means. What is this investigation they are working on? And what do they want with me?

"I want to speak with Tripp Jackson, Assistant Director with the FBI and I want to speak to him now." He got no response from them in the driver in the front seat.

Two miles further down the road, they pulled onto a dirt trail and Robson said, "End of the line for you, Ryan."

Chapter Thirty-One

Nick noticed a large mobile command center parked in a nearby clearing, abuzz with activity. Once out of the car, they told him to have a seat underneath a broad canopy stretching from the back of the huge black-and-tan RV vehicle. He rubbed his wrists and hands to regain some circulation.

The tall one said, "Sit down. You're going to be here for a while."

Ryan stood and demanded, "If you won't get Assistant Director Jackson on the line then I want to speak to whoever is in charge. And I want it now." The two men looked at each other and one retreated inside the trailer.

He glanced at his watch and waited until the door of the trailer opened and a tall man walked down the steps and came towards him.

He offered his hand, "Mr. Ryan my name is Kender, Jon Kender. I'm with the ATTF and the agent in charge of this investigation concerning a number of plane crashes that have been happening." He showed him his ID as Robson stood beside him, watching.

"Can somebody tell me what's going on here?" Nick asked

"Have a seat, Mr. Ryan. Just give me a moment," he said as he intently looked through a manila folder before looking up to address Nick. "Tell me what you know about catawampus."

That again. Two days ago, he had never heard the word before, and now he hated the sound of it.

"Agent Kender, first of all I want to point out to you that I'm an agent with the FBI in good standing and I am more than willing to tell you whatever you want to know but I don't appreciate begin dragged here by your men as if I were some common criminal. I'm on leave from the FBI and have a very close relationship with the Assistant Director, Tripp Jackson. I'm sure if you picked up the phone and called him he would be happy to vouch for me."

"I'm sure Mr. Ryan. In all due time, but your personal connections are not what we are interested in tonight. Again, Mr. Ryan, it is very important for you to tell us everything you know about catawampus. That is the only thing that I'm interested in now. Please." His tone softened.

"Not much really. I was leaving my home in Delray Beach, Florida to come to a funeral of my brother-in-law in Baltimore, and before I left a woman approached me and asked me to help her look for her missing brother."

"What's her name?"

"April, April Kenyon."

"Go on."

"Well, she gave me a picture of him and her and information about his last-known whereabouts."

"Where was that?"

"Somewhere in the Caribbean. She also told me about where he worked and told me the last thing she had heard from him was a one word text message—catawampus."

Kender leaned in closer at the mention of the now-hated word. "And...?"

"That's it. She asked me to look into his disappearance, so I've been asking around to see what I could find out, but so far I've come up empty-handed. I called her missing brother's boss and asked if he knew anything about Kenyon's disappearance or had ever heard the word."

"You mean Matt Scott at the *Herald*?"

"Yes," his eyes lit up. "I guess you've talked to him too, but he didn't know anything about it either."

"He's dead, Ryan. He fell to his death this afternoon from his parking garage."

"But I just talked to him today."

"We know." He leaned closer to Ryan. "So tell me the rest of the story Ryan. What does it all mean? Catawampus? I find it a coincidence that you start asking people about Catawampus and they wind up dead."

Nick bolted from his seat and stood nose to nose with his accuser. "What are you trying to imply? I love my country and those who live in it, and I would never, ever do anything at all like that. Now you either charge me with a crime or release me. Now!"

Robson held his arm, holding him back, "Sit down, Ryan," he commanded.

Kender paused, looking at him, sizing him up. "Wait here," as he walked to a convoy of black SUV's approach them from the street. A group of men got out and Kender was walking back to him, joined by a tall, thin man in a pinstripe suit. It was a familiar face.

"Hiya, Nicky," his old friend Tripp Jackson said.

"Hey, Tripp. What's going on? I told Kender here everything I know. Is this the case you told me about at Tony's funeral?" That time seemed like years ago.

"Yeah. This catawampus thing really threw us off." He paused before asking, "Kender, you got some coffee inside." Kender nodded his head and they all walked towards the command vehicle. "Nicky, you want some coffee? This may take a while."

"Yeah, sure," he said glancing at his watch.

"Join me inside; I wanna show you something."

The interior of the van was filled with radios, computer screens, and banks of telephones. Assault gear and weapons lined the walls with a small working desk at the very rear. The sounds of an exhaust fan noise whirred in the background, providing little relief from the still night air.

"Nick, what I am about to tell you is extremely sensitive and has not been seen by anyone outside of the taskforce."

Nick's curiosity was now aroused as he sat down at one of the nearby chairs. "I understand, Tripp."

He exchanged glances with Kender who stood by the desk and nodded his consent and said, "Mr. Ryan, we are questioning everybody that has a link to this Catawampus. I am sure you understand."

"I understand completely. I…"

Kender interrupted him before he could finish. "Jackson here also tells me that you are one of the best intuitive investigators he has ever seen, which is a very high compliment coming from him. I myself believe we spent a lot of money on all this high-tech equipment to give us the answers we need, and we would be better off using, it but we are at a dead end."

Tripp added quickly seeing his old friend becoming annoyed, "This investigation is under the complete control of the ATTF. The FBI is here only in an advisory role. Everything we discuss here, Nick, is incredibly sensitive. You can imagine the panic it would cause to the American public if they knew there was somebody out there knocking down our airplanes. Air travel would grind to a halt and this country and maybe the world economy would see a recession like it has never seen before."

Nick nodded his head. "Got it."

"Let me show you something." He picked up a manila envelope and carefully pulled out a clear plastic folder with a letter inside and handed it to Nick. In large block letters, he read the following:

GREEDY AIRLINES—
YOU DID NOT BELIEVE ME, AND PEOPLE DIED.
YOU VALUE MONEY MORE THAN PEOPLES' LIVES
AND NOW IT IS GOING TO COST YOU MORE OF BOTH.
THE PRICE HAS GONE UP TO $20 MILLION DOLLARS IN
DIAMONDS.
PLACE IN LOCKER NUMBER #499 AT HEATHROW AIRPORT
OR PEOPLE WILL DIE.
DELIVERED TO ME NO LATER THAN 12:30 P.M. TODAY
CATAWAMPUS

Nick read it twice before handing it back to Tripp. "I see why my inquiries about catawampus set off a lot of warning bells. Do you have any leads on this?"

"No. We have had all of our profilers, the best forensics people, and trained linguistics people, each giving us nonstop insight. They are telling us that this and other notes were written by a male, age thirty to forty who is not a native English-speaking person. In addition, we did not find fingerprints anywhere. It was printed on everyday copy paper with a laser jet printer most probably non American. We're checking into that lead as well."

"How was it delivered?"

Couriers delivered them to different airline headquarters addressed to their CEOs. No surveillance photos and the payment information was delivered by another courier usually on a bike. Nobody has seen this phantom. He probably has multiple layers of cover to shield him."

Nick picked up the note again and examined it more closely. "Do you have the other notes?"

Kender reached into the safe behind him and retrieved the other documents handing them to Nick. "Here's the first one."

GREEDY AIRLINES—
YOU HAVE RIPPED OFF THE AMERICAN PUBLIC FOR THE
LAST TIME. NOW YOU ARE GOING TO PAY FOR YOUR
GREED.
I WANT $1 MILLION DOLLARS IN LOOSE DIAMONDS
DELIVERED TO LOCKER # 36 AT SUVARNABHUMI

*Kender said aloud to no one in particular, "We checked all the lockers he
wanted us to do the drops in, and none of them had false backs or bottoms. He had
to know we would be watching these lockers. He can't be that stupid thinking he
could just waltz in and pick up his ransom. It has to be something else. What are
we missing?"*

Nick leaned back in his chair and sipped on his fifth cup of coffee
saying, "Well, I don't think we're missing anything. He wanted this last
ransom to be delivered by what time?"

"He said it had to be delivered by 12:30 P.M."

"And the plane crashed at what time?"

Kender pulled the file from the binder on his desk, "Let me see, let
me see," he said, pulling out a legal pad. "It crashed at 1:47 P.M."

"So he had no intentions of taking the ransom and stopping the
plane from crashing. There was not enough time; his plan was already
set in motion. He was just toying with you." They were all silent trying
to see if they could glean any other clues from the ransom notes.

"What was the name of the first airport where he wanted the
diamonds dropped?" Nick asked, sitting forward in his chair.

"The *Suvarnabhumi* airport in Thailand."

"He's laughing at us. *Suvarnabhumi* stands for *the laughing one* in Thai.
What about this missing former mechanic who was seen near the plane
before it left Rutland?"

"Stugen? We have the Canadian Mounties looking for him as well as
the local police where he usually goes for his hunting trips. Everybody
is searching for him. The Canadians and border patrol have over two
hundred law enforcement people on his trail plus a hundred FBI
agents. We'll find him. He is still considered a person of high interest in
this investigation until we rule him out. Yes, he could be our guy or
could have seen our guy messing around with the plane. We don't
know and are trying to keep all of our options open. We are still trying
to find out the actual cause of the plane crash anyway."

"Why did he ask for diamonds?" Nick wondered out loud. "I know
that they are untraceable and it's easier to carry diamonds than $20
million dollars in cash, but why diamonds? Unless it's just another way
to stall, knowing that it would take quite a while to find $20 million in
diamonds. My gut instincts tell me this guy has something else in mind,

a much bigger plan. And we may not find out what it is until it is too late."

"What do you mean?" asked Kender, pouring more coffee.

"I mean if he's not interested in the ransom then what does he want? This guy is twisted, but from what everything I've seen, he has it all planned out. And what is the implication of the use of the word, catawampus. And does the death of Matt Scott have any connection with your investigation?"

"More questions then we have answers I'm afraid," Tripp chimed in. "But we have over three hundred federal agents working on it. Now that the President has taken a personal interest in this, he's asked me to coordinate all the various agency efforts."

"That's good. But I still wonder, what does Catawampus mean?" Nick asked.

"We have found a lot of meanings but the most common is something that is crooked or out of alignment. Cross-eyed?" responded Kender.

"But there is another, more sinister meaning—fierce, destructive; a fierce imaginary animal, a bogeyman," added Tripp.

"Does he or she see themselves as the tip of the spear so to speak? Or perhaps as an avenging angel?"

Nick looked at a map stretched out on the wall. The crash site was circled along with other places of interest. He noticed a small historic chapel also listed nearby. He studied it intently. "Do you have the site map from the first crash?"

"Yes, I do."

"Can I take a look at it?"

"Sure, let me get it for you."

He unrolled it on the long table. "Here is where it went down," said Kender pointing to a large green X marked on the map. "What are you looking for, Nick?"

"I'm not sure exactly," he responded, without looking up. Then he saw it: a parochial school less than a half mile away from the first crash site. "Target practice."

"What do you mean?"

"Somehow he's bringing these planes down, and not to confuse the issue, but maybe he is zeroing in his sights for his final target. And then using the ransom demands to throw us off track."

"You're nuts, Ryan. Go home and get some sleep."

"It's just a SWAG, but this guy has something bigger in mind, and all of this is just target practice."

"What the hell is a SWAG?"

"A Scientific Wild Ass Guess," responded Jackson from the corner of the room, taking it all in.

"Well, hotshot, if you know it all, what is this guy's target that he is practicing to hit? Huh?" asked a sarcastic Kender.

"Just giving you some additional input that's all, Jon. And I'll tell you something else…"

He was interrupted by a knock on the door, "Special Agent Kender, we got 'im!" said a young agent in orange jumpsuit. "The Mounties just notified us that they caught Stugen in some lakeside cabin with tons of explosives. He initially confessed to the aircraft downing's but now won't talk to anybody and is lawyering up on us. They've already started extradition proceedings on him."

Kender clapped his hands at the news. The pieces of the puzzle were slowly starting to fit together.

"Get some men up there and question him. I don't want to wait on this. Let the NTSB know as well. So much for your greater target conspiracy theory, Ryan."

"This is one time I don't mind being wrong, Jon," smiled Nick. "I would like to follow up with you after you have him in custody just to tie up some loose ends. If that's all right with you."

"OK Nick, but remember anything I tell you is off the record and unofficial until the official report comes out. Got it?"

"Fine by me. Thanks." Nick stretched his neck and arms to help keep him awake. It had been a long night. He could see the sun rising over the hills behind them through the still-open door.

"Good seeing you again, Nick. I'll be briefing the director and the president soon," said Tripp.

"Yeah, you too, old buddy. But I think it's time for me to go. If I can get a lift back to my hotel from one of your guys, I'd really appreciate it?"

"Yeah, no problem, Nick. Thanks for your help and input," he said as he shook his hand.

It had been a long day and he was tired. Riding back to the hotel in the big SUV with the sun rising in the sky he began to wonder. *What am I going to tell Megan?* How could he explain what had happened to him and still keep it confidential? He would just tell her the truth, whatever he could share, and hope she would understand.

Chapter Thirty-Two

Nick plopped onto his bed at the hotel without undressing and slept for hours; when he woke he knew it was time to call Megan. He called her house at nine o'clock and got no answer. He tried again at 9:30 then again at 10:00 o'clock. Next, he tried to reach her at her office, no luck.

As Nick left his room he saw the package from the overnight delivery service leaning against the wall. He flipped it over and saw it was from April and found her note inside:

> *Nick—*
> *Here's my brother's paperwork that I promised to send you. Hope your assignment is going well in Vermont and you'll be back soon. I look forward to seeing you and getting together with you when you return. I have a lot I want to talk to you about.*
> *Warm regards,*
> *April*

Nick set the package down. *Life was getting complicated.* He pulled out the paperwork she had sent him and found a stack of handwritten notes, receipts, bills, a map, a manila folder with the word Catawampus and a question mark written beside it. The sweet smell of her perfume lingered in the air.

The alert mind of an inquisitive detective was running at full speed as he went through the meager folder and realized none of it made sense. The notes talked about missing government billions and the search for even more of the missing funds. The word Catawampus and Tiger Eyes were printed in large block letter. *Missing money? Billions? Catawampus? Tiger Eyes?* He did not know what to make of it. *Del had said in his message that he was on the trail of a lot of missing government money and his body had turned up off the coast of some small Caribbean island. This all had to be tied together.*

After he had showered and dressed, he returned to the paperwork and spread it out on the bed. It still did not make sense to him.

He noticed the rental car keys on the counter with a note from the hotel telling him where the car was parked. He drove downtown, and saw her as she walked towards the small bakery on the main street of Woodstock and hurried to catch up with her. Her back was to him, and he reached her just as she was opening her car door.

"Meg," he said to her.

She turned, and the hurt look in her eyes said it all. "What the hell happened to you last night? No, on second thought I don't want to know. Just leave me alone." She stood across from him and looked away but he could tell she was hurting.

He paused. "Meg, let me explain…please."

She turned, venting her full fury on him, "The same old Nick. Still afraid to make a commitment, is that it? You'll never change. You did this to me before, and now I remember why I told you I never wanted to see you again. Just go Nicky, please, just leave me alone and never come back," her voice trembled as she turned her face away from him, and the tears began to swell in her eyes. Looking at him she said, "My heart said to love you Nick, but the rest of me said to let it go and just live with the memories."

He touched her shoulder.

She trembled at his touch, "No…don't… please. Just go Nick, go back to Florida."

His cell phone rang. "Nick. Hi, this is Tripp. Wanted to let you know, we located Stugen and interviewed him in Canada… he's not our guy. Yeah, he's got a big chip on his shoulder for being fired and all, but he's not our man."

"Why do you think that?"

"We got another note and another crash. No way he's our man. This time it crashed off the coast of Florida. The newspapers, the radio and TV people are all over it. It's getting way out of hand. The agency and ATTF is on its way along with the NTSB, but we don't think there are going to be any survivors. There were over two hundred people on that plane Nick."

"Oh my, God," he moaned, placing his head in his hand.

"I could use your help. Can you get back to Florida?"

He was now fully alert and focused. "Sure Tripp, I understand completely. When do you need me there?"

"As soon as you can get here. Kender's plane is still in Rutland, and it's bringing him back here today. It leaves in an hour. Can you make it?"

He looked at his watch and took in a deep breath," Yeah, I can make it."

"Good. He'll brief you on the plane and have you fully up to speed by the time you get here to Florida. We're dealing with a real nut, but a real cool customer and he's not done yet."

"OK. I'll meet him at the plane and we can leave later together late. Where do you want to meet?"

"We're setting up a command post in Key West. We are taking over the Oceanside Motel on Duvall Street. I'll meet you there. Gotta go."

"All right, Tripp. See ya' soon."

"OK, Nick. Thanks. Oh and before I forget... you were right. He was practicing. He hit a lighthouse on a small island just off the coast right before they crashed."

"Sometimes I hate being right. See ya, Tripp."

He turned back to face Megan.

She paused for a minute before asking, "So you have to leave?"

"Yes," he said solemnly as he glanced at his watch. "But this is not as I would have planned it, Meg. Not at all. You understand, don't you?"

"I know you have to go. You will always have to go...somewhere. Perhaps it's for the best. What would you do in sleepy little Vermont?"

"I'd have you."

"I love you Nick Ryan. Go find whoever you need to find and when you are ready, come back here. Come back when you finally know what you want. I'll still be here."

Ringggg...ringggg. His phone rang again with its insistent ring. They both breathed a deep sigh of resignation.

"Yeah, Tripp?" he asked his old friend, trying to make the call as brief as possible to spend the last few moments he had with her. He was falling for her again; he knew it, and now all he had to do was to convince her.

"Hello? Nick?"

He froze, it was Katie's voice. "Katie?" he asked in disbelief.

"No. Is this Nick Ryan? This is April Kenyon."

"April?"

"Yes. Sorry to bother you, but you said to call you when I got back in town. Well, I just got back to Delray today and wondered if we could meet sometime. I would love to see you…and…well; we could go over what you may have found out about my brother's disappearance."

His mind raced. *This will teach me to look at caller ID before I answer the phone.*

"I'll be getting back into town tomorrow, but I'm going straight to Key West for an investigation."

"The plane crash?"

"Yes. How did you know?"

"It was on all the news channels tonight."

"Oh. I haven't been watching the news."

"Nick, I got a phone call from my brother or at least a call from my brother's phone. The voices were very muffled, and I had a hard time hearing anything. I couldn't really tell anything. Nick, I am so worried about him. It's not like him at all."

"I won't have much free time until I find out what is going on. But once I do, I'll call you and we can go over your brother's disappearance. If that works?"

"Yes, that would be great. So you'll call me?"

"Yes."

"Talk to you then, Nick. Goodbye."

He hung up the phone and turned to see Meg walking away.

Chapter Thirty-Three

The sleek gold and white government Jetstream GS-890 lifted off hours later from a private corporate airport runway outside of Rutland, Vermont. As they settled into the wide leather seats, Bender handed him a folder with updated information about the crashes.

"Two hundred and sixty-eight people were on that plane, Ryan. Two hundred and sixty-eight innocent people had their lives ended in an instant at the whim of some lunatic. That's what drives me in this job, to stop crazy people like this." He paused for a moment showing a rare sign of emotion.

"I want this guy Ryan, and I want him bad," he said in a chilling voice. "I have to tell you I wasn't in favor of bringing you into this case but TJ thinks you're the best and that's good enough for me. Read through this folder, then we'll talk."

He opened the folder and began to study its contents. Some of it he had seen before at the crash site in Rutland. He continued to leaf though it while asking, "Any further insight into the meaning of Catawampus?"

"None. It's a puzzle, but one that we must solve. Our only clue was the reference you gave us… but that could have been a coincidence. Who knows?"

Ryan grunted in acknowledgement but silently disagreed. *He didn't believe in coincidences. Never did. Which told him that the two cases were linked somehow? But how and more importantly, why?* He looked out the window and in the early morning light saw the bucolic Vermont countryside drift by below and he thought of Megan. He could not get her out of his mind. It was then he realized how special she was and how much she meant to him. *He missed her already. Focus Ryan.*

From his worn leather briefcase, he pulled out the paperwork that April had sent him to help provide clues into her brother's disappearance. It included expense reports, scribbled notes, past stories he had written, and telephone bills. On the bottom of one piece of paper was written Catawampus. The word was circled, and then in smaller letters, it was written again but split into three words Cat-a-wampus. *Why?* He moved to show it to Bender.

"This is where the reference to Catawampus came from in the case I was working on," he told him.

"I see. That's all?"

"Yeah, that's the only clue I have."

"I'll pass this on to the lab boys and see if they can glean anything from it." A photo fell to the floor beside his foot. Bender reached for it then handed it to him saying, "Nice-looking woman, Ryan."

He smiled. It was the picture of April she had given him. She looked just like his Katie, smile and all. His mind drifted back to the times that he and Katie had shared together. Good times. Happy times. Those were the times he treasured. He smiled and fell back into his seat and slowly closed his eyes. He knew he had choices to make, choices that had to be made whether he liked it or not.

Her hand touched his hair like she always did, pushing it back behind his ear. He could smell her perfume, the soft scent of jasmine. He reached forward to taste the color of her lipstick. So inviting. She smiled at him. The devilish twinkle in her eye reminded him of home. It was so good to see her again. God how he had missed her. Katie. April. Megan. Katie.

"Ryan, wake up we're coming in for a landing. Put your seat back up." It was Bender. The folder was still on his lap. The city lights shone bright beneath them. "Those are bright city lights for Key West" he said, looking out the window.

"It's not Key West—it's Baltimore. We've been ordered to make a stop here at Fort Meade, NSA."

"Who did that?"

"POTUS, the President of the United States," responded Bender dryly as the corporate jet came in for a smooth early morning landing.

Chapter Thirty-Four

Two black Chevy Suburbans with Maryland license plates beginning with BJ were there waiting for him. The plates only confirmed to Nick that the Secret Service was now involved. What was their involvement he wondered as they drove towards the NSA Headquarters just outside of Baltimore?

The NSA headquarters building located on the grounds of Fort Meade Army base was tall and imposing. The agency was the lifeblood of electronic intelligence for the United States. Adjacent to it was the new headquarters building of the United States Cyber Command, NSA's equivalent of an attack dog.

Where was this investigation going? And more importantly why was he still involved? Ryan asked himself. He only came up with one word a word he now hated. *The only good thing was his insurance company client was off the hook, and now all he wanted was some time to clear his head and think about Megan and April. But now, that did not look like it was going to happen. What next?*

The car pulled in front of the massive headquarters building. Bender and Nick were whisked in behind two armed guards, up an elevator into a large glass soundproof room when he was introduced to the people attending. Four men were already there waiting for them, sitting around the long mahogany wood conference table. A man in a dark suit and tie with an American flag on his lapel was seated in the corner, observing.

They were introduced to the Director of Cyber Command, Jack Jackson and Deputy Director, Matt Rowe. A tall thin man was introduced as James Holmes, the Director of Intelligence Operations at NSA and Luke Garrison, Staff Intercept Section Manager. Everyone was introduced with the exception of the man in the corner.

Holmes stood and came right the point. "Gentlemen, we have strong reason to believe that these plane crashes we have been experiencing are not equipment malfunctions but rather a targeting of our civilian aircraft. I would like to have NSA's Senior Specialist, Mr. Luke Garrison expand on that. Mr. Garrison."

"Thank you, sir." Luke stood and looked around the room. Now he remembered why he liked working with computers instead of people. He was terrified of talking in front of a crowd. He stammered for a minute to catch his breath and continue. He swallowed hard. He froze and the words did not come out. He looked around the room for help until he saw Ryan give him the thumbs up and seeing it gave him confidence to continue.

"Just as the director mentioned," he started, coughed, then cleared his throat and reached to take a gulp from the glass of water sitting in front of him. He began again, "I have found that there are two burst of data prior to a crash. The amount of time between the first and the second burst of data ranges from minutes to hours. The timing of the data blasts we identified have coincided with the timing of the plane crashes."

"Pure coincidence," Bender interjected. He stood and asked the young techie, "Are you trying to tell us that sending a data stream to an aircraft will bring it down."

"Yes sir, if it's done properly and if the data stream is strong enough."

"Why do you think there are two bursts of data? And can just sending data to an aircraft cause it to crash," Bender interrupted again.

"One blast is an identifier or in the trade it is called a handshake to make sure that it has identified the proper target. Once locked on the rest is easy."

"Hell, I wish we had a weapon like that," said Holmes.

Director Jackson looked at him but remained silent.

"Finally, we feel that this work could only be done at the direction of a foreign government or somebody with a lot of money to spend on some very sophisticated equipment, or both."

Ryan took it all in but kept still. This was not his show. He was merely an observer. He admired the young guy because he stood his ground.

The room burst into a cacophony of competing voices. Each man was trying to be heard over the other, arguing the points that Luke had just made.

The unidentified man in the corner stood and the room became silent. "Mr. Ryan can you excuse us for a few minutes, please," he asked softly but with authority. "Mr. Garrison, would you be kind enough to show Mr. Ryan here where you discovered all of this interesting information. We would like to have a private discussion if you don't mind."

"Yes, sir. Follow me Mr. Ryan, please."

The bickering started again before they had even closed the door behind them.

"Luke, call me Nick. Everybody does. Tell me about this data blast."

"Well I can't take the real credit for it; my computer did all the work. She discovered the pattern."

"She?"

"Yes, we have become very close, if you know what I mean," he said with a smile and a wink. "I'm glad they gave you the purple high-level security badge that lets us go just about anywhere in the building. Otherwise you would be confined to lobby and first floor-access only. Follow me."

The computer room was the largest Nick had ever seen, twice as large as the ones at the FBI in D.C. "We have sixteen rooms like this scattered throughout the NSA complex. It would take something nearly this big or larger to do what I proposed in the conference room. This was not something you can do from your home computer, at least not yet anyway. But the technology is moving faster and faster all the time."

"What exactly are we talking about, Luke?"

"The Data Blast sends so many signals to its target and to the onboard computers that it gets overwhelmed and in a defensive measure it shuts itself down. It is really doing it for its own protection. Real simple concept it just gets more complex when you try to implement it."

Luke pulled up a chair in front of a computer terminal. "Sara, hi, this is Luke. Do you have any information for me?"

"Hi, Luke. I've missed you. Can you stay awhile and talk or is this all business?"

"Sorry, Sara, but this time it's business." He looked at Nick and whispered, "I told you we were close."

"I see."

"Sorry, I can't take you around and show you the really neat stuff, Nick, but even with a purple badge I have to confine you to this room. But Sara here can do just about anything you would want. Go ahead ask her anything you want. Sara, this is my friend Nick."

"Hi, Sara."

"Hello, Mr. Ryan."

"How did you know my last name?"

"I did a digital voice scan and matched it to our records. I also checked our login data at the front desk and a Mr. Nicholas Ryan was admitted forty-five minutes ago."

"Cute. Sara, what is the deepest part of the…"

"Come on, Nick," Luke interjected, "that's an easy one. The deepest part of the ocean? Come on, ask her something tough. Maybe a case you have been working on?"

"OK. Sara, tell me what you know about Catawampus."

"What?" Luke said in amazement.

"Catawampus. A friend is missing and the only clue I have is the word Catawampus. OK? Sara, tell me everything you know about Catawampus."

"Catawampus, two items of recent history. One, Catawampus was a highly controversial breeding program started by Doctor Erhard Schmidt where he cross-bred wild ferocious animals for unknown purposes. His breeding program was halted in Zambia in 2011 when rebels burned down his camp and released all animals. His current whereabouts are unknown, but he is thought to be somewhere in the North American hemisphere."

"Hmmm. Sara what was the second reference?" Nick asked.

Silence.

Luke repeated the command, "Sara, what was the second reference to Catawampus?"

"That reference is classified, Level 10—White. No further information is available."

Luke looked perplexed. He had never had a response like this before.

"It's OK, Luke. Ask Sara what the plane crashes have in common, outside of the ordinary and usual."

"Oh, she loves questions like that. Sara?"

"Yes, big boy."

"What do the following crashes have in common, outside of the usual manufacturer and the like?" He read her the dates of the crashes and they could both hear the massive computer spinning and collating the data. The high-speed printer began to belch out reams of printed commonalities.

Luke took in a deep breath as he read the planes had similar tires, sparkplugs, lighting equipment, brakes and onboard computers with a listing that stretches on and on covering six thousand printed pages. It cross referenced the backgrounds of the passengers, staff, crew and maintenance personnel. The list appeared almost endless.

Luke was not about to be foiled and then asked, "Sara, give me the most interesting list that you found in your search."

A single sheet of paper was deposited in the computer printer tray.

LUKE—ONE CREW MEMBER FROM EACH PLANE HAD PRIOR WORK EXPERIENCE AT IRAQI GLOBAL AIRWAYS

"Interesting, very interesting," murmured Nick. "Luke asked her for the employee names and when they worked at Global."

Again a single printout was delivered.

"Luke, I have another request. It's kind of personal one."

"Shoot Nick, old buddy. My lips are sealed."

"I'm looking for information on a missing person. I'm searching for the current whereabouts of a man by the name of Sean Kenyon."

"Sara, what can you tell me about Sean Kenyon, especially his current whereabouts?"

The computer's light began to flash and the machine began to shake and hum.

"I have a listing on 16,000 persons listed under the name Sean Kenyon. Further data clarification needed."

"Nick, do you have the guy's address, phone number, social security number anything?" Luke asked trying to be helpful.

"No…only that he worked as a reporter for the *Saint Louis Herald* and has a sister named April. She said she just got a phone call from him but I don't have his cell phone number."

"Computer what targets do you have with the prior information?"

"None listed in Saint Louis under the name of Sean Kenyon; however, I do have one listed under the name of Michael Sean Kenyon in Clayton, Missouri, a suburb of Saint Louis."

"That could be it," said Nick.

"If we had his cell number we could do some really cool things. Are you sure you can't get it?"

"Security took my cell phone for safekeeping when I came into the building. Wait, wait let me check my briefcase. I have some of his expense reports and notes and a phone bill." He laid his briefcase on the desk and began sorting through it.

"Here we go; here's his cell phone number," and handed it to Luke while he continued to search through the young reporters motes.

"Great." The young techie took over manual command of the key board and began typing furiously. "Nick, I see he used his cell phone in the last forty-eight hours but not to make a call—to take a picture."

"What? How can you tell?"

"I'm with the NSA, remember? All we do is listen in and monitor peoples' conversations, emails and other communiqués. It's all we do. Give me just a minute and I will tell you where he is."

"How?"

"All these smart phones have a built-in GPS that tell you where you are. Well, that works both ways; it can also tell the world where you are. If you know how to look." Luke punched numbers into the keyboard then leaned back in his chair. "There he is, Sean Kenyon is...in the Caribbean."

"How can you tell?" asked Nick, his eyes transfixed on the screen.

"His phone is activated. See the flashing beacon on the screen? That's your bud, Michael Sean Kenyon. He is located on a small island in the Caribbean called Little Jamaica which is between Little Cayman Island and the island of Jamaica."

Nick was amazed at this information. "Let's call him. I need to talk to him."

"Let me try," asked Luke.

No answer but the beacon light on the screen continued to flash.

"Here are some other numbers he called. Look at this string of numbers he wrote down. Try calling this one," Nick told him pointing to a list of numbers on the notepapers as he dialed Sean's cell phone.

Luke laughed. "That, my friend, is a phone number but your friend, Sean Kenyon used an old reporter's trick. It is the first thing you learn when you become a cub reporter. I was a summer intern at a local newspaper. You see, if you're working a lead and have a phone number, you write it down backwards so nobody will find out your contacts. It sounds simple but it works. "

He laughed as he held the sheet filled with notes and numbers. "Let's see what we have if we reverse the numbers..., 202-355-493..."

Nick froze when he saw the phone number. *Why hadn't he noticed it before?* The phone number that Luke wrote down gave him chills. He knew that phone number; it belonged to his dead brother-in-law, Tony!

What the hell was Sean doing in touch with Tony? Sean was missing and Tony was dead. And Del's body was fished out of Caribbean waters. What was the connection? What did Sean know about Tony's death? What was the connection with Del's murder? Now he wanted more than anything to talk to Sean Kenyon, and the sooner the better.

"Call him again."

"Still no answer." Sean's phone continued to ring.

"He has it blocked or there is no signal."

"But we're getting a beacon signal? I remember his sister said he doesn't always answer his phone."

"There is always a satellite signal for the beacon, but most times it isn't strong enough to make a call."

Nick paused then turned to his new friend and pleaded, "Luke how can I find him? And quick!"

"Just follow the beacon."

"How do I do that?"

"I'll send you an application I created. When you get outside you download it to your Smartphone."

"You made it?"

"Yeah, I call it Stalker. After you download it, just follow the blinking beacon on the phone to its location on Little Jamaica, that's all. Tell you what, give me your cell phone number and I will send you the link to the app. Then all you need to do is to activate it."

"You can do that?"

"Nick, how many times do I have to tell you..."

"Right, right... you're with the NSA. You know this would be a great app for people to find their cell phones when they have misplaced it."

The young techie made a face, "It would never sell, trust me I know what I'm talking about. But this little gadget is going to make me a lot of money for people looking to track down a girlfriend or boyfriend and prints out a list of every stop where the person stays longer than a few minutes."

The phone on Luke's desk rang a loud but insistent ring. Luke picked it up and listened before saying, "Yes sir, we're finished here. Yes sir, I'll escort him back to the front desk."

He looked at Nick, "That was the director's office. We have been summoned. They're ready for you and want you to wait for them at the front desk. Come on, I'll show where you can pick up your phone and other personal belongings."

Nick's mind was whirling with the information he had just heard and still trying to piece it all together.

I have to find Sean Kenyon. But how? I'm going to Little Jamaica and find Sean and find out what happened to Tony and Del?

Chapter Thirty-Five

Indonesia Air military cargo flight #MT-948, prepared to take off from the Singapore Changi International Airport at 11:23 P.M., the last flight out for the evening from the huge international airport.

The tower called, "Come in MT-948, you're cleared for takeoff on runway two-niner."

"Thank you tower, y' all have a good evening now, ya hear," responded Captain North a native Texan and the senior pilot in the fleet.

Once the airplane was aloft, the military escort trucks on the runway returned to the terminal. They were finished guarding the loading of the high explosive munitions aboard the big jet and see it safely take off. Their job was done, it was safe as it made its way to the buyer in Australia.

"Once cleared from our airspace don't forget to turn your transponder back on, MT948. Do you copy?" the tower boomed inside the cramped quarters of the jumbo jet.

"Yes, we do tower. That's a roger. See you on our way back."

North turned to his co-pilot, Useff Gurin, "Give it a couple of minutes until we clear their airspace and then switch on the autopilot and then the transponder. Then wake me in two hours," and slumped down into his seat for a long overdue nap.

"Yes, sir," said the young co-pilot looking over his shoulder and saw the small Cessna two-seater trailing behind them as they made their way to their Australian destination. "Autopilot engaged, sir."

"Good."

The plane was now on track to its predetermined destination.

"You can turn the transponder back on now," he said a few minutes later without lifting his cap from his face.

"Oh captain, look outside to the left and tell me what you see."

The pilot lifted his cap and leaned as far back as he could but saw nothing. "It looks all clear to me Useff. I don't see anything out there at all but..." he turned back to his young copilot who had a small-caliber pistol pointed at his heart.

"What the hell are you...?" he shouted. Useff pulled the trigger and the middle-aged pilot was dead in an instant. He wobbled his wings to signal the Cessna to pass him as he took it off autopilot and headed due west. The two-seater turned on an identical transponder and headed south towards Australia. There was no pilot in the cockpit of the small plane as it plunged into the sea some five hours later. That is where the entire world would search for the big jumbo jet and never find it.

Under the cover of darkness, the huge cargo plane landed a few hours later on the Cocos Island and was immediately whisked inside a large hangar on the south side of the remote island. The final piece of the plan was now set in motion.

Chapter Thirty-Six

"I'm afraid this is going to be the end of the line for you, Agent Ryan," said *Robson dressed in grey suit with an American flag on his lapel. "Mr. Bender will not be joining you. The plane will take you home to West Palm Beach, but then it has been diverted to MacDill Air Force base to pick up some people. Director Jackson said I can tell you these airplane bombings are now a national security Level One priority. That is all I can tell you. Thank you for your input. And we must also ask that you refrain from further pursuing any leads regarding this airplane business."*

"I understand," said Ryan in a voice that sounded only half-truthful.

"Sorry about that Nick. Have a good day, Agent Ryan," he said with a short grin before turning away.

Once airborne Nick turned on his cell phone and saw the message from his now good friend Luke and clicked on the link. He activated the app and punched in Sean's cell phone number and the beacon from Sean's phone began to beep. He was watching it glow, and it seemed stationary on the tiny little Caribbean island of Little Jamaica.

He then saw a link to some pictures taken with Sean's cell camera. He clicked on the link. The first picture was of an old rundown airport. The second was of a hotel with a sign on the front the proclaiming it the Little Jamaica Hotel. The third picture was of some trees with a big white house beyond it. The last picture was an eerie nighttime shot of glowing yellow, orange, and black eyes. Gleaming eyes. Hungry eyes. He was mesmerized by the evil eyes glowing back at him. *Tiger eyes?*

The phone shook in his hands as it rang. It slipped from his fingers and dropped to the floor. He watched it slide out of sight as it rang again. He reached for it but was held back by the safety belt. He reached again, then finally released the clasp from his seatbelt. "Hello," he said nearly out of breath after his ordeal.

"Nick? Nick...is that you?" he heard a familiar voice say. "Hi it's me, April."

"April?" he said thinking her voice was a perfect match for his Katie. "How are you?"

"I'm good. I don't mean to bother you, but I thought I would see if you were able to find out anything about my brother."

"Yes, as a matter of fact, I have. Some good news I think."

"Really! Tell me more, please. I can use some good news," she said in an uplifting voice.

"Well, I tracked his phone to an island in the Caribbean called Little Jamaica."

"Little Jamaica? I'm not familiar with it."

"It is part of the Greater Antilles island chain, which includes Grand Cayman Islands, Jamaica, Haiti, Puerto Rico and others."

"That's great! I'll call him right away."

"Well that's the bad part. It is on an island that gets little or no reception. Very weak signals. I can only track his cell phone whereabouts. I'm on my way there now to check it out."

"Where are you?"

"I'm on a government jet that lands at West Palm Beach International in a little over two hours. I'm going to book a flight to Jamaica and then catch a puddle jumper to Little Jamaica. I'll have more news for you tomorrow. Just hang in there. OK?"

"No, it's not OK. I'm comin' with you."

"What? No! Absolutely not. It's too dangerous. April, please trust me on this, please. I promise I'll call as soon as I found out anything. I promise. Really, this could be very dangerous."

Silence.

"OK, I hear you," she said, the disappointment obvious in her voice. "Call me when you find out something."

"Will do." *It was like talking to his Katie. The same bubbly enthusiasm, same obstinate nature, and same devilish sense of humor, but his Katie would have never given up so easily. Maybe she wasn't exactly like his Kate, after all?*

The phone rang again. "I told you I would call you as soon as I found out something. Just trust me that…"

"Nicky?"

"Pop?"

"Yeah. When the hell were you going to call your old man and tell him you're still alive? I keep hearing about these plane crashes and that's all they're reporting about on the radio and television."

"I was just about to call you, Pop, honest."

"Bullshit! What's going on? I don't hear from you for days on end, and I start to wonder about all the bad things that can happen, especially when all these planes are falling out of the sky. Where are you?"

"I'm following up a lead on who may have killed Tony."

"Well, your Uncle Nick, your namesake, is coming in from Oregon this weekend, remember? For my birthday? I finally got him to agree to come visit us."

"That's great."

"Yeah. And don't forget you promised you'd be here with me to celebrate. This is the… 'Big' birthday for me… but hell at my age they're all big ones. Nicky, I'm counting on you to be there."

"I'll be there, Pop, count on it."

"I am. Well, listen…I want you to be real careful. Whoever murdered Tony has killed once, maybe more and won't hesitate to kill again. You hear me?"

"Yeah, I hear you. I'll be careful and I'll call you in a few days. There's little or no cell phone service where I'm going."

He was going to find Sean Kenyon, and then maybe he could get some answers and find out who killed Tony. And Del. But for now, one step at a time.

Chapter Thirty-Seven

Tuesday afternoon, and the open-air market was hot and dusty in the Iraqi city of Fallujah with the noonday sun blistering overhead. The city was bustling and traffic had returned to normal from the three-day holy day over the previous weekend. Young girls from the nearby secondary school shopped together in small groups as they playfully walked down long alleys of the open air market. The mosque across the street had just finished noonday prayers and the men searched for a cool place to have their lunch.

Sitting unnoticed just off the main square, hundreds of meters away a man sat in the front seat of an old green four-door Peugeot sedan. The car was stolen the night before in Baghdad. Those passing by would later not remember him much less be able to describe him to police. His fingers, with beads of sweat dripping down his fingers, impatiently tapped the top of his leather briefcase which lay on the passenger seat. He checked his watch again for the tenth time. It was nearly time, just a few more minutes.

Two young boys passed him on their way to the market; they should be ready soon. They were the last of his team to be in place. He had trained them and the others for days on what they had to do. Mr. Tuesday had dropped four at the police barracks, three at the hospital, and the final three at the mosque. He called them his holy twelve, and because of them this would be a Tuesday the whole world would remember. Now he just had to wait and listen. This was the worst part for him. He looked at his watch... it was time. He closed his eyes to fully experience what was about to happen.

The earth shook as the huge explosion rocked the tranquility of the early afternoon and when he opened his eyes he saw the huge red fireball fill the sky followed by a mushroom cloud of dust and debris rising above the city. It was a couple blocks away but he could see large clouds of smoke billowing from the fire below and knew that the age old market was destroyed along with everyone inside. He glanced at his watch. Eight minutes. Time.

Again, the ground shook as he turned to look through his rear window at the mosque some six blocks behind him being engulfed in flames. Right on time. The second hand on his watch ticked away the minutes, tick—tick—tick. It was getting louder, louder than his heartbeat. The adrenaline flowed through his veins. His watch counted the minutes.

He was so close he could hear the sounds of sirens and frantic cries for help. His breath came faster and deeper. Ambulance and fire rescue vans rushed to the scene. The final bomb blew with the greatest intensity and the windows of his car rattled from the intense shock waves as it rumbled through the streets. He swallowed hard and closed his eyes tight again. His heart beating faster and faster all the while. Straight ahead at the police station, he saw the red fireball fill the air. Chaos filled the small city of the desert.

More. He wanted more. He checked his watch. Minutes passed in what seemed like hours. *Patience. They would all be on scene by now, helping clearing away debris and bandaging those they could help.*

Time.

His fingers pressed the metal clasps on the side of the briefcase and unlatched them. They sprung open briskly upon his command. He raised the leather top and slid aside the piles of dollars and *Riyals*. He removed the remote control and set it on his lap. His finger was on the switch counting 3…,2…, 1! He closed his eyes and pressed the button on the detonator. In mere seconds the city was filled with the sounds and cries of the largest explosions it had ever experienced. The sound of the sirens stopped and he turned the key to start his car. *Time to leave, time to get ready for next Tuesday.* His breathing was slowly returning to normal. *Time to go.* Next week promised to be a busy week for Mr. Tuesday.

Chapter Thirty-Eight

July 2014

The huge Saudi Airlines jumbo jet roared off into the night sky leaving Dulles Airport and the lights of the nation's capitol lingering below it. The plane settled into its flight path to Jeddah as the captain turned the red autopilot switch to the "on" position. The next time he touched a control would be to taxi the plane to the airport terminal in the desert kingdom and disembark its eight hundred passengers.

When the aircraft reached its cruising altitude of thirty-two thousand feet the cabin attendant announced over the intercom to passengers who all listened intently to her message.

"Good evening ladies and gentlemen, and welcome aboard flight #1278 from Washington D.C. to Jeddah, Saudi Arabia. Our flight time is approximately fifteen hours and forty-nine minutes. We will be coming through the cabin with warm towels and taking your dinner orders in the next fifteen minutes." A beep sound interrupted her monologue for a brief moment.

"The captain has turned off the seat belt sign, and you are now free to move about the cabin. We do suggest however suggest that you keep your seatbelt fastened when seated in the unlikely event we encounter some turbulence during our flight. Thank you, and enjoy your flight."

The cabin soon began its transformation. Men who had boarded the plane in business suits untied their ties and removed their jackets and began donning traditional pilgrimage garb. Women lined up to use the bathrooms as changing rooms. They entered dressed in skirts or slacks and emerged wearing long white traditional garbs. The metamorphosis lasted for over an hour, and at the end the steady hum of religious prayer chanting could be heard throughout the plane. They were on their way to the largest annual pilgrimage in the world, the calling of the faithful. They were heading to the holy pilgrimage in the holy land.

They would join an estimated three million other travelers at the holiest site on earth to their religion.

The massive plane with its cavernous cargo holds was filled on this journey by special shipments destined for the desert kingdom. The hundreds of large wooden crates set off the detectors at the airport but were not inspected due to the diplomatic labels plastered conspicuously about the large crates. The security personnel were more concerned with shipments coming into the United States then those leaving the country.

Midway over the Atlantic Ocean the copilot noticed a blinking warning light on his control panel. It blinked once before going out. *A faulty or loose bulb,* he thought to himself. He thumped it with his forefinger, and it came back on.

This flight was going to be another dull transatlantic run, he thought to himself. They would fly to Jeddah but only after doing a traditional ceremonial fly-over of the holy site. Then land in Jeddah before the return flight to the United States. This was the captain's last flight for two weeks. He was going on a long-needed vacation to the Bahamas. Yes, that was worth waiting for, he thought to himself as the routine flight continued on its journey east.

• • •

Late that night on the outskirts of Wichita, Kansas a military KC-135RT Stratotanker refueling aircraft was being loaded with jet fuel. Its crew was doing a final checklist for its regular weekly training run from McConnell Air Force Base traveling south past Oklahoma City before turning back north to return home. This time, however, the plane would be fully operational carrying over 200,000 pounds of aircraft fuel and was to undergo a nighttime mid-air refueling exercise.

A cockpit light blinked off then immediately back on, unnoticed by the nearby crew. The plane was ready to depart on its mission.

Chapter Thirty-Nine

The sleek government Gulfstream jet glided in for a smooth landing, as it barely kissed the sweet earth below and rolled down the runway to the private corporate jet tarmac at West Palm Beach International Airport. Nick Ryan grabbed his bag as exited down the steps and headed for the ticketing counter for Air Jamaica.

As he walked though the airport he saw more security then he had ever seen before, with armed guards, bomb sniffing dogs walking through the airport inspecting anything suspicious. He saw other armed security personnel guarding the planes on the ground. Every television he passed was tuned to local and national news about the recent planes crashes as people watched in silent worry.

He noticed the Air Jamaica ticket counter up ahead to his left. "Good morning. When is your next flight to Kingston?" he asked the young uniform attendant behind the counter.

"Good morning, sir. Let me check. Our next flight is schedule to depart in one hour."

"I'll take one ticket, please."

"I'm sorry, sir, but that flight is sold out. I do have room on our flight leaving the same time tomorrow."

"Does anyone else fly to Jamaica?"

"Yes sir, but the earliest flight from any of them is tomorrow night. I'm sorry, sir. Would you like to book tomorrow's flight sir with Air Jamaica?"

Nick thought for a moment trying to sort through his alternatives before speaking, "Well, if that's all that's available, I guess I'll take…"

A soft voice behind him finished his sentence, "He'll take a pass. Thank you."

Katie?

He turned to see April standing behind him, waving two airline tickets. "The early bird gets the worm so to speak. I booked us both for today's flight. I also booked a puddle jumper flight to Little Jamaica and a rental car when we get there," she said with a determined smile. "We leave in an hour. Want something to eat?" She walked away, as he watched her hips slowly swaying to the sound of a silent slow Caribbean melody.

He ran to catch up with her. "I thought I told you it was too dangerous for you to come along. Didn't I?"

"Yes, you did," she said and kept walking. "And I told you I was coming. As a matter of fact, I'm leaving today. If you don't want to come with me then you can wait for tomorrow's flight. What will it be?"

She had him boxed in, just like Katie always did. "All right, all right, you win. But I'll take the lead when we get on the ground, OK? You hear me? Deal?"

"Deal," she said with Katie's smile.

He could not stop looking at her. It was as if he was in a dream and never wanted to wake up.

"Hungry?" he asked passing a small concession stand.

"Famished," she said.

"Grab a table, and I'll see what they have. Be right back," he said as they approached a small carry out stall.

He returned with a food tray and sat down across from her at the table.

"Not much to choose from as you would imagine. But here you go. For you a garden salad, a chocolate croissant, and a *café au lait* just the way you like it. And for me a coke and a cheeseburger."

"What do you mean just the way I like it? We've never had ..." she made a face looking at the coffee cup and taking a sip said, "Is there any coffee in this? I like to taste my coffee. I think they forgot it," she said reaching for the sugar. "But this chocolate croissant is decadent!"

"Like it?"

"I love it."

"I knew you would."

"Pass me the sugar," she asked.

"Sugar? You never drink sugar in your coffee." *Nick, Katie didn't take sugar but April... get a grip.*

She reached across the table and touched his arm, "What do you mean, I never take sugar? Nick, I think we need to...," She was interrupted by his cell phone ringing.

"Hold that thought," he told her as he walked away to take his call, it was Luke Garrison.

"Hey Nick, sorry to bother you, but I thought you would want to know we got two more handshakes, but one of them is different this time."

"What do you mean...different?"

"Well, the first one was like all of the others but the second one was a much weaker signal as if it came more from a local transmission or..."

"Or what?"

"It had the signal strength of a cell phone or personal computer. But that's crazy. It just doesn't make any sense."

"Yeah, I agree but I'm curious if they got another letter from the madman."

"I don't know but our target focus has increased a hundredfold here. I got fifty techies working for me day and night on this thing. Something big is going on. Hey, I gotta go, the bosses are back. Talk to ya later," he said in a rushed tone.

While he waited for his order to be completed every television screen he could see were filled with stories of the plane crashes. Reporters and anchors were espousing their own views of who was behind it and what should be done. The entire nation was on high alert, and from the interviews on TV they were scared.

As he walked to the table he saw her sitting there looking more like Katie all the time. She shook her hair to get it off her face the same way she always did. When she smiled, her single dimple lured him to her big beautiful eyes. When he sat down across from her, an announcement came over the airport intercom:

AIR JAMAICA FLIGHT NUMBER #1842 TO KINGSTON JAMAICA IS NOW READY FOR BOARDING. PLEASE PROCEED TO THE GATE NUMBER SIXTEEN AND PRESENT YOUR BOARDING PASSES TO THE GATE ATTENDANT. THANK YOU. ALL ABOARD AT THIS TIME.

"April, it's time to go," he said. "Let's go find your brother."

Chapter Forty

It was three A.M., and he was in no mood for more bad news. "Did we get another note from our maniac bomber?" the president asked, now fully awake and alert.

"Yes sir, but you're not going to believe this one Mr. President. He's asking, no he's demanding that all terrorist bombing in the Middle East be stopped for one week; otherwise, he will unleash the sword of Damocles on the world. This guy is crazy."

"Crazy like a fox. Call our National Security Council here for a meeting in one hour. Now."

"Yes sir."

An hour later in his office he fingered the latest message from the terrorist in his hand, shaking. His chief of staff stood nearby. "Here it is Mr. President,"

GREEDY PEOPLE—
YOU STILL DON'T BELIVEE ME WHEN I TELL YOU PEOPLE
WILL DIE.
MY FAMILY WAS KILLED BY TERRORISTS AND NO ONE
CARED.
YOU WILL WEEP TEARS OF BLOOD IF YOU DON'T DO
WHAT I COMMAND.
TELL YOUR FRIENDS TO STOP FUNDING TERRORISM.
STOP THE BOMBINGS A WEEK BY MIDNIGHT
OR
THE SWORD OF DAMOCLES WILL BEFALL ALL OF YOU
AND NOW IT IS GOING TO COST YOU MORE.
THE PRICE HAS GONE UP TO $500 MILLION DOLLARS IN
DIAMONDS.
PLACE IN LOCKER NUMBER #499 AT HEATHROW AIRPORT
OR PEOPLE WILL DIE.

DELIVERED TO ME NO LATER THAN 12:30 P.M. TODAY
CATAWAMPUS

He swallowed hard. "Get me the Saudi Ambassador on the phone. Pronto."

Chapter Forty-One

The Little Jamaica airport runway was filled with ruts and potholes and barely long enough for the small ten-passenger Air Jamaica propeller plane to land. It stopped just short of the end before being confronted by a jungle of large overgrown wild impenetrable line of bushes. They waited in Georgetown, Jamaica for six hours before continuing on to the tiny island of Little Jamaica. It was dark by the time they flew into the tiny airport on Little Jamaica, on the smallest island in the Caribbean.

"Welcome to Queenstown, the capitol city of Little Jamaica," spouted the voice of the friendly captain. "Those of you who are looking for a fine place to stay during your time on our wonderful island I can be happy to recommend some fine places run by my family." The airport building was nearly deserted with the exception of three men in white shirts carrying pistols shoved inside the waistbands of their trousers. The men sat smoking cigarettes and watched them walk by mumbling something in a foreign tongue before laughing aloud with toothless gums. April reached for Nick's hand and squeezed it tight for support. She gulped and smiled feebly. "Maybe I should have stayed in Florida."

Their rental car had seen better days, and an unknown dashboard light flashed red as they pulled away. It continued flashing as they drove away from the airport and on their way into town. Nick had to re-acclimate himself to driving on the "wrong" side of the road from the "wrong" side of the car on this former British colony. He pulled out his cell phone and touched the Stalker app button. The beacon light began to flash a weak, blinking light.

"Straight ahead, Nick," murmured April taking the phone from him, her eyes now fixed on the flashing light.

The dirt and rock filled road was bumpy and the dust from the street at night made it impossible to see. Streetlights were nonexistent until they made their way into what appeared to be the city center.

"Turn left at the street corner," April told him. "And slow down. We're getting close." A pack of wild dogs ran across the street in front of the car causing Nick to slam on his brakes. The car stalled and would not restart. He tried again.

"Let's walk. It doesn't look to be too far ahead," she said looking at the flashing beacon. The car doors would not lock.

They walked a couple hundred yards with strange sounds and smells coming from the small huts that lined the road. "There it is. I recognize the picture from Sean's phone," she said excitedly, staring at the phone before breaking into a run.

"April wait, let's be cautious until we know what we're dealing with OK?" he hollered after her.

She kept running, and when she reached the steps of the hotel, it was deserted. The hotel's front screen door creaked as she opened it and after looking down at the phone she climbed the inside steps to the second floor. They squeaked as she ran up the stairs, jumping two at a time then down the upstairs hallway stopping before room 211. "April, wait!" Nick pleaded. The beacon flashed bright and fast as Nick ran to catch up with her.

"April, stop! Don't go in!" Too late, she turned the knob and her sisterly welcoming smile disappeared. Three large Jamaicans dressed in white suits seated in the torn leather green easy chairs greeted them. The tallest one held a pistol in one hand and Sean's cell phone in his other.

Nick was right behind her.

"Good evening, mon. Welcome Agent Ryan. We have been waiting for you to join us," said the tall one waving the gun for them to sit down.

"See, I told you we should have waited," she said.

Yeah. Nick managed a small grin, but his mind was processing the information searching for a plan of action.

"Don't try anything foolish, Mr. Ryan. This is our island. Understand?"

"I understand." *What's next?*

"Welcome to Little Jamaica, Agent Ryan. Follow me."

Chapter Forty-Two

The tall one slid into the front seat of the big black German SUV and motioned for them to sit in the rear. They pulled away from the empty rear parking lot of the ramshackle hotel and headed down the main street. They bounced from one side of the car to another as the driver drove as if he were driving in a road race. Fifteen minutes later, they turned off the main thoroughfare and drove down a paved single-lane private road. They stopped at gate and he read the sign:

NO TRESPASSING
KEEP OUT!
CATAWAMPUS

There was some spirited discussions among their captors until the tall man yelled at the youngest one. It was something in Creole Nick did not understand. The youngest one got out, unlocked the gate, and swung it open. The SUV rushed in and stopped, allowing the youngster to lock the gate and quickly re-board the car. Something there spooked him judging from his nervous laugh and fast talking dialog with his friends. They drove for another fifteen minutes and a second gate appeared.

"Fast, mon! Now," said the big Jamaican to the young one. The younger one jumped out of the car and ran as if evil spirits in the dark would grab him at any moment. He waved his hands fast to push them through and climbed back aboard. This time there was no joking amongst them when he rejoined the front seat. His hands were shaking.

Nick nudged April and pointed to the large white house ahead. It was the house they saw from Sean's phone. Up close, the house was an old white French Colonial that even in the dark was obvious that it had been restored and meticulously maintained. At the front door, they were greeted by a butler dressed in a crimson green jacket, speaking perfect English, "Good evening, Mr. Ryan and Ms. Kenyon. My name is Mevans; please follow me. I will have one of the men retrieve your luggage. I have directed them to return your rental car the airport. You will have no further use for the automobile now that you're our guest." He was tall with wisps of white hair on the side of his head. His long narrow face was sunken in just beneath his eyes, making his eyeball sockets appear recessed.

"And whose house is this?" she asked.

He turned, his face nearly the color of his jacket reflecting his embarrassment, "Oh I'm so sorry. Where are my manners? You are the guests of Mr. Ahmed Koshari. Would you like to be escorted to your rooms? Perhaps to freshen up after your tiring journey?"

"No, thank you. I want to find my brother! Why does that man have my brother's cell phone? I would like to see Mr. Koshari now. I have some questions for him. Please."

"Ma'am, Mr. Koshari is not available at the moment but will be soon. I am sure that he is also very interested in speaking with you. May I show you to your rooms?" he asked leading the way up the grand staircase without waiting for a response.

Their adjoining rooms were quite large with priceless modern art adorning the walls. Nick checked the windows, locked and barred. The huge canopy bed filled a large portion of the room. He heard a knock and went to the adjoining door.

"Nick, are you in there?" he heard her ask.

"Yes," he said and turned the knob, the door swung open.

"God, how could I be so foolish? I should've listened to you." She put her arms around his waist and pulled him close.

Nick could feel her heart beat and smell her sweet perfume. He ran his fingers through her hair.

"All the windows have bars. And the fence we passed outside was electrified. Nick, I'm scared."

He looked at her and kissed her, finding her wanting, melting in his arms. She kissed him. Now it was his heart beating faster. *Don't take advantage of the situation, Nick.*

He pulled back, "Everything will be fine, April. Trust me. I think...," there was a knock at the door.

"Yes?"

"Dinner will be served in one hour with cocktails in the study with Mr. Koshari in thirty minutes. Please be prompt. Your luggage is here should you wish to change."

"Thank you, Mevans," she said.

"See you in twenty minutes?" she whispered to him. "I'll knock."

"OK," he said kissing her on the cheek. *This could be our last night together*, he thought—*with a madman!*

Chapter Forty-Three

"Mr. President, the Saudis have denied all involvement with financing any terrorist activities but promised to see what they can do to talk to their comrades and help stop the funding of all the bombings for at least a week. But they made no promises."

The tall lanky commander-in-chief sat at the head of the table with all of his top advisors in attendance. "They always deny involvement with anything to do with the terrorists. God, don't they know we have positive proof of them paying these guys to run around and blow up mosques and schools."

Mike Trost, the President's chief of staff chimed in, "They just want to keep the *Shiite* and the *Sunni* fighting against each other rather than attacking their own interests in Saudi Arabia. But they are just so transparent about it."

"Enough. Everyone here has been briefed on this lunatic bomber. Do we have any leads at all on this guy who calls himself Catawampus? Is it a person, a group … a movement? Come on, people, give me what you have."

"Mr. President, we have thousands of leads we're pursuing on this…," added the director of the CIA, Ron Carson.

"I mean viable leads," the president said icily. He wanted answers, and he wanted results. "Ladies and gentlemen, we can't have some nut going around and blowing up our civilian aircraft. People will be afraid to fly, and then we'll have a real economic mess on our hands. Jackson what does the FBI have?"

"Mr. President, we are closing in on a few very viable leads. We have interviewed over thirty thousand informants and as you can imagine we have made this our top priority. As best as we can tell, this is a lone individual acting alone, a little crazy but alone… with a lot of money. All the things he does cost money, tons of money."

"Anything else? Any other leads?"

"Mr. President, sir, we have been trying to keep name, Catawampus out of the newspapers. The public is scared enough as it is with the planes falling out of the sky for no reason. But we have had leads coming in from all over the globe. Even agents on leave have reached out to us, like Nick Ryan."

"Ryan? Good man. I remember him when the FBI was working with the Secret Service on a presidential protection coverage work he did for us. What's his take on all of this?"

"Well, he was working on another case and the name came up a couple of times with regards to a missing person file. I have calls out to him, and I am waiting for a callback."

"Check it out since it sounds as if we have very little else to go on. Gentlemen, we meet again in four hours. I have meeting scheduled with the Israelis, the British, the Canadians, our NATO allies, the Russians and the Chinese. Hell, were even reaching out to Hamas and the other terror networks. Next time we meet, you'd better have something for me. Good day, gentlemen."

Tripp Jackson turned to his director of field operations and whispered urgently, "Find me Nick Ryan. Pronto!"

Chapter Forty-Four

She appeared at his door dressed in a pair of black slacks and a small gold chain dangling from her neck while a touch of light colored lipstick flavored her lips. She looked incredible. It's amazing what women can fit into a small leather attaché overnight bag. *Nick glanced at her sideways as they prepared to join their mysterious host for drinks and dinner. She was a knockout and for some reason everything seemed so normal, so natural.*

He slowed down their walking for moment and said, his voice turning serious, "April, I want you to follow my lead tonight. We're dealing with a madman and anything can happen, so, I don't want to rile him up or get him angry. Anything could happen then. Trust me, we'll get all of our answers but with a maniac like this, I think it's best if we just let him talk. People like this love to brag about what they have done. He'll tell us everything we need to know. If not, then we'll just ask him outright. Act like it is a perfect evening and he is the perfect host."

She started to say something but he stopped her, "We'll find out about Sean, believe me. Okay?"

She looked at him, squeezed his hand in hers and said, "It won't be easy but I'll try."

His hand went to hers, and she squeezed it ever so softly as Mevans smiled at them as they came into the study.

"Good evening. What may I prepare for you?"

"April?"

"Mevans…, I'll have white wine spritzer please for me."

"Of course. Sir, for you?"

"I'll just have a glass of red wine."

"Yes sir, coming right up."

The room was large and lavishly appointed with deep dark wood paneling covering the walls. Expensive artwork hung everywhere; a large polar bear rug lay in front of the sofa. The double French doors led to a patio with a garden beyond it. The scene was breathtaking with the ocean waves crashing just past the boulder break wall, the water turning to immense white frothy waves as they crashed upon the rocks. Lights on a neighboring island appeared in the distance. To Nick, it looked like the perfect escape route.

"It appears that one could jump from the rocks and swim to that island over there," said a voice behind them. "That would be a good plan except for the sharks. This is their natural feeding and breeding grounds. Many men have tried it only to wind up as dinner for our scavenger friends out there."

Nick turned at the sound of the voice.

"Good evening. Allow me to introduce myself. My name is Ahmed Koshari. My family is from Iraq but this part of the world is now my home. Excuse the fortress like appearance of my home but like all very wealthy men, I have many enemies. I do ask that you stay near the house unless you are traveling with one of my escorts on the grounds."

Mevans served the drinks and their host raised his glass to say, "A toast to health!"

"Cheers," responded Nick, as the observant detective eye surveyed his surroundings and noticed the armed guards manning the doors trying to appear as nonchalant as possible.

"Speaking of which," April blurted out, "I want to know…," Nick squeezed her hand and interjected. "We would like to know how you knew we were coming to the hotel in town?"

"Well, we found this cell phone in our security zone and we saw the texts which came from your phone and your name was listed in caller ID. The signal is not strong enough for commercial calls from this island, but it does emit a signal."

"Where's my brother?" April finally demanded, shaking Nick's restraining hand.

Showing his annoyance Ahmed said, "You will be reunited with your brother in due time."

"He's OK then? I've been so worried about him. Can't I see him now?"

"Soon," he said with a forced smile.

"But…,"

"All in due time, Ms. Kenyon, all in due time."

"Dinner is ready," Mevans announced from the doorway.

"Please, let us enjoy the evening. We don't get many visitors here," Koshari implored.

"This is home then?" Nick asked as they walked into the main dining room. The long dining table was large enough to easily seat thirty people comfortably.

"Oh no, this is but a retreat for me. The main house and my offices are both in Georgetown on the Grand Cayman Island. Please have a seat. Mevans is a wonderful gourmet chef and has prepared a wonderful dinner of duck soave drenched in caviar for us. But no need to be formal tonight, please sit here, near me at the head of the table then we don't have to shout to one another. We are very civilized here."

Nick sat next to April, but he could tell she was terrified and wanted answers. He placed his hand on her leg to stop it from bouncing up and down. He knew this man was dangerous, and as refined as he appears he would not hesitate to kill them. He turned and saw the guards still at the door.

Ahmed noticed his discomfort and waved the guards away. "Better?" he asked.

"Yes, thank you."

"They are very protective of me here. Please excuse them."

The meal and wine was very good but Nick was anxious to find out the answers to his questions.

"Now, I am sure you have some questions for me, so please, ask away."

"Why did your men kidnap us in town?"

"Oh, I think using the term *kidnap* is a little harsh. You are free to leave at anytime. You must excuse the over eager conduct of my men. I have grown accustomed to their very vulgar and blunt ways. I apologize, although their old island habits are very effective. Wouldn't you agree?"

"I suppose."

"Did you say we are free to go?"

"Why of course, however the sentry animals which guard the perimeter are on the loose so it would not be safe on the grounds without an escort."

"Sentry animals? Catawampus?"

Their host eyed this American in a new light, his eyes narrowed, "Yes, Catawampus. Bravo, Mr. Ryan."

"That is a unique term, but I've heard it used quite frequently in the past week or two."

Koshari's face showed his disappointment. "Pity Agent Ryan, I was just beginning to enjoy your company and that of the lovely Ms. Kenyon, who I must say looks absolutely ravishing tonight."

"Catawampus?" Nick asked again. "We saw the sign as we came in the main gate, Beware of Catawampus."

"Ah yes. It is the end result of ill-fated experiment that I financed. You see there was a South African geneticist by the name of Doctor Erhard Schmidt. He did some crossbreeding in Zambia, Africa until rebels overran his camp in 2011 and chased him out of the country. I offered him funding and the use of this island retreat to continue his experiments." Nick could tell he was enjoying an audience for his stories.

"He was cross breeding spotted African hyenas with tigers. Unfortunately, many of the crossbreeds went crazy and the hyenas' tendency to survive killed most of the remaining tigers with only the strongest surviving. Unfortunately for Doctor Schmidt he was not one of them. Two got loose in his lab one night, and well…it was very bloody to say the least. They are quite vicious. The lab is in the basement of this building. Would you care to see his creations?"

"Not at this time," said April, closing her mouth as she took in a deep breath. A madman.

Ryan was persistent but treaded lightly; he realized that the man sitting in front of him was the man everyone was chasing – Catawampus. He was crazy. "Mr. Koshari, there have been many instances of aircraft being downed and the notes claiming responsibility for it have been signed Catawampus. Any thoughts?"

"Agent Ryan, I think it is time we stop playing games, don't you? I find it an extraordinary coincidence that a highly respected FBI agent knocks on my door and pretends not to know anything about my connection to what is happening around the globe." Suddenly, blood began to ooze from his nostrils, dripping down the front of his white suit. His face and eyes appeared to be changing color and texture right before their eyes. He grabbed the napkin and held it to his nose to try to stop the bleeding. It was no use.

"Mevans!" he screamed. "Mevans!"

"Coming, sir," the manservant said as he burst through the doors while holding a hypodermic needle. "It will only take a moment, sir, patience."

"Goddamn it, Mevans, you know I have no patience for this. Why the hell do you always tell me to have patience? Damn it, man, what are you waiting for? Get another one ready like the last time." Nick and April saw their well-mannered host transformed into a raving lunatic in a matter of seconds. They exchanged telling glances.

"Yes, sir, but you know your tolerance for these shots is not very good."

"Don't argue with me! Goddamn it, Mevans! Don't just stand there man—get it! Get it now. Do I have to do everything on my own?" The second shot seemed to quiet him and stop the bleeding. Nick could feel the shivers in April's legs as she watched him turn into a madman. Her eyes were wide with fear. She was a combat-hardened doctor but had rarely witnessed such symptoms and changes in personality. "You may want to go to a hospital and have that looked at," she whispered.

While changing his shirt behind a bamboo privacy shield in the corner he said from his seclusion, "I have seen many doctors around the globe, but they can't help. I already know what it is—uranium poisoning. I am dying from it, that I know for sure, if I don't go crazy first."

"Uranium? From where?"

"It is a long story, but since we aren't going anywhere this evening, I guess we have the time. Mevans, please bring some cognac for my new friends in the study."

"Yes, sir. I will clean this up later," he said setting down the bloody napkin.

The study was a much smaller, more intimate room with a sofa and two large leather chairs arranged around a large fireplace. Moments later, Mevans appeared carrying a silver tray with crystal glasses and proceeded to pour a glass for each. Nick swirled the glass in his hand as he intently watched his host. The cognac burned warm down his throat. One French door was open on the far side of the room and the sheer curtains floated about the room from the sea breeze outside. April slid next to him on the sofa, the warmth of her leg touching his. It was still shaking. A howling noise outside echoed in the distance.

"Where to start? Let me see."

"How about starting with Tony Galvechio?"

He laughed. "Ah, yes. I nearly forgot about him. Let's go back further. Growing up I adored my mother and idolized my father. However, my father was left to die in a burning building while the local religious leaders rescued books and let my father die in the flames. I vowed revenge, but I didn't want to do it on a small scale. I wanted to make everyone feel the pain that I felt when I lost him. You see, I planned and plotted it for years and then the American invasion of Iraq provided the perfect opportunity. More cognac, Mr. Ryan? Ms. Kenyon? Mevans!" he said, raising his hand high above his head.

April continued to glance at the open French door at the other end of the room while the white satin sheers billowed inside by the night wind. The room was getting cooler, and night howls continued to fill the evening air outside with the sinister sounds of rustling leaves... and something else.

Mevans silently appeared from the other room to refill their glasses. "Coming sir." They heard a loud and long howl outside the door. After pouring drink refills, he closed the double door and pulled the long green velour drapes across the opening. April heaved a sigh of relief but could not shake the feeling of a strange presence outside- it was terrifying.

"Better?" asked Koshari with a slight smile.

"Yes, thank you," she said holding the cognac now in between both hands.

"Where was I? Ah yes, after my father died I was homeless, unemployed, and an outcast since I was schooled in the west and spoke perfect English. Someone not to be trusted by most Iraqis. It was a curse until the Americans arrived. After they bombed my homeland into oblivion they flooded the country with a virtual tidal wave of cash, huge mountains of greenbacks. Tons of cash! It is estimated that the United States sent over three hundred sixty tons of one hundred dollar bills. It is impossible to comprehend. Billions upon billions of untraceable and unaccounted for American Yankee dollars flooded into Iraq. So, I arranged to be there to count the money going into the warehouses and also arranged to ship it out the back door. I pocketed my own billions. But so did everyone else... just not as much as I liberated." He laughed then downed the rest of his cognac, signaling for a refill from his manservant before continuing. He did not get many guests here and he was relishing the time with them.

"Well, I sent all my money overseas to my special accounts in the Caymans, next I bought oil tankers and storage facilities here, in the Caymans and throughout the Caribbean. I secretly became the largest buyer of Iraqi oil at less than a dollar a barrel. The Iraqis didn't care since the money went right into the pockets of the bureaucrats and the Americans didn't care because the money had come from Saddam Hussein's private accounts. Billions! And remember, for every two million barrels of oil taken off the market it increases the cost of gasoline by ten cents a gallon. Doesn't sound like much does it? But what happens if that oil is taken off the market and just sits. Its value goes up and up and up."

He laughed at his own inside joke.

"It cost me nothing to buy the oil, next to nothing to store it and the value goes up every week. So I just kept buying and shipping barrels of oil, millions of barrels. I filled all of my storage facilities, and then I bought cheap tankers and parked them off the coast of the Caymans and waited. Soon, I had a couple hundred million barrels of oil and the price of oil and gasoline just kept going up. Next I used my billions to purchase oil future contracts. I could control billions more barrels of oil."

"I'm sorry, but what does all of that have to do with us?" asked Nick.

"Sorry, I got off the subject. Well, the U.S. government hired me to ship and fly old equipment out of Iraq… then they wanted me to fly GI's home and elsewhere. So I bought planes and made even more money. They ultimately asked me to dispose of depleted uranium shells and they paid millions more. I began to stockpile radioactive shells as the final part of my plan took shape. But you see, my problem was twofold, some of the pilots who flew for me in Iraq heard of my plan and got greedy. They blackmailed me; they wanted money, millions of dollars for their silence. I could not do anything overt so…,"

"So you began knocking the planes they were on out of the sky under the guise of some terrorist demanding ransom?"

"Exactly! You are a very bright lad Mr. Ryan. "

"But why not just have them killed? Why did you have to kill innocent people in the process?"

"Collateral damage. You can understand that can't you?"

"You were practicing crashing a jet into a target, weren't you?"

"Well yes, Mr. Ryan, yes I was. This is exciting. Go on Mr. Ryan, please don't stop." He dabbed his handkerchief to his nose.

"You have all this oil, you have a planeload of radioactive uranium, you hate the religious groups in the Mideast, you hate the United States so…, so how do you take your revenge on all of them at one time?"

"Don't stop, Mr. Ryan, you are so close. Please." He was excited.

"You somehow take control of a plane and crash it into an oil field in Saudi Arabia, causing massive disruption in the oil flow which then makes your oil that much more valuable.

"Yes? And…? What else Mr. Ryan?"

Ryan looked stumped. "I don't know. Let me think."

The man stood before him egging him on.

"What next Mr. Ryan? What next? You're a bright man, think!" he screamed.

It suddenly became clear to Nick. He looked him in the eye and said calmly, "You don't crash it into an oil field at all... you crash it into a holy place where there will be millions of religious followers worshipping from all over the globe... the pilgrimage! Of course. You don't want the oil destroyed, you just want it neutralized...and the holy site would be radioactive for a couple hundred years and so would their oil. And my brother-in-law was just a pawn doing his job when he stumbled across your oil and money thievery and started looking into what happened to the missing billions of dollars. If word leaked out about you before you could implement your plan you would have to find an alternative plan. Correct?"

"Yes, Mr. Ryan, but to bring down the first couple of planes I needed an army of computers to take it down so I must thank my North Korean friends in Pyongyang. I couldn't have done it without them but now with my own specialized software once they put it on autopilot I can take control of any plane I want as if I were at the controls inside the cabin of the plane. Then I reprogrammed autopilot, just like an onboard GPS system you find on those fancy American cars. However, you see, I now have two options at my disposal. These high school kids are incredible with the stuff they come with aren't they? Their programs and their apps, marvelous. They are so ingenious. Mevans, please ask Cole to join us here in the study."

"Yes," they whispered in unison. The mad man continued to rant but the two guests sat and listened overwhelmed by the sheer lunacy of his plan.

Nick volunteered in saying, "But the United States will immediately activate its Strategic Underground Petroleum Reserve in Louisiana and it is underground so your plan will only be a minor setback. But that would take weeks to mobilize. So..."

"Yes, go on, Agent Ryan. You're on a roll. How exciting."

"So crashing a plane into the strategic reserves really doesn't help. It has to be someplace where oil is in storage or in the petroleum network for it to be of benefit to work for you and...the only place that would really cripple the economy would be a disaster at a place like... Cushing."

"Bravo, bravo, Mr. Ryan. You get a gold star. I see now why you are one of the FBI's top investigators."

"Cushing? Where's Cushing?" asked April.

"Cushing, Oklahoma. It is where over twenty percent of our country's oil is stored and distributed nationwide," Nick told her glumly. "An explosion there would be devastating to the entire United States economy. It would take years to recover, and the price of oil worldwide would hit unheard of highs," he mumbled to himself thinking of the consequences of this madman's actions.

"But it would make all of my oil as valuable as gold," Ahmed grinned, "and the North Koreans would have first access to it for assisting me."

Mevans soon entered the room with a slightly built young man wearing sneakers and a torn t-shirt. He looked at his watch impatiently.

"Ah yes, Cole. Welcome. Mr. Ryan, allow me to introduce you to my tech wizard, Cole McLean. With his help, I now have two methods to bring down my planes. You see, I like backup plans. Cole reprograms the planes and then I notify my friends in Pyongyang to send a massive overload of data to cripple the plane but now thanks to Cole here we can be much more precise and do it from his personal computer or his cell phone. Ingenious, isn't it?"

"I didn't think you could get cell phone service here?" asked Nick.

"That is correct except that I wasn't going to let that little detail stop us from our completing our mission. Cole, why don't you give them a quick overview of your ingenious little app and then we must hurry off?"

The young techie began in a high-pitched voice and explained, "I can hijack an airplane's navigation systems using a smart phone app, radio transmitter, and flight software I purchased off the internet on eBay. I developed this game which works in real life called, PlaneSploit which uses the Flightradar24 live flight tracker and you can tap into any airplane in the air."

Nick nearly laughed aloud, "From a goddamn cell phone? You must be kidding?"

The young techie pulled out his Smartphone to demonstrate how he could adjust the heading, altitude, and speed of a virtual airplane by sending it false navigation data. "You can use this system to modify everything related to the navigation of the plane and that includes a lot of nasty things." He looked pleased with his explanation.

"My smart phone app named Plane-Exploit, takes advantage of a plane's Aircraft Communications Addressing and Report System (ACARS), which uses short transmissions to beam data between aircraft and satellites. ACARS has no security at all. None. It was never needed, before this. Anyone can transmit fake data to alter an aircraft's trajectory. The airplane has no means to know if the messages it receives are valid or not. So they accept them all and you can use them to upload data to the airplane that triggers these vulnerabilities. And then it's... game over." He grinned at his accomplishment not realizing the reality of his newest toy.

"Many people will die innocent people. Don't you care?"

Ahmed intervened, "Ladies and gentlemen, I have details to attend to for our big moment, so I am afraid I must leave you now. Tomorrow at breakfast, you will wake to a new world order. Goodnight." A drop of blood dripped from his nose onto his shirt.

"Wait!" April nearly shouted, "You said you would take me to my brother. I have waited all night like you asked but now I must insist that I see him."

"I don't think you really want to see him," he said, raising his hand and pointing to the rear yard of the house. "We buried his body in the back of the house along with other interlopers. He was trespassing on my property and had the misfortune to have a run in with our hyenas at the fence. They are vicious and very protective attack dogs. I'm so sorry, Doctor Kenyon. I would ask that you stay in your rooms tonight please or you may have the same fate. Mevans will show you to your room now. Goodnight."

Chapter Forty-Five

Nick heard her crying and knocked on the door, which separated their rooms. "Are you all right?' he asked through the door. "I wanted to make sure you're OK."

She opened the door and when she saw his face she threw her arms around his shoulders hugging him. "He's a raving lunatic. He killed my brother, my brother who never harmed anybody in his life. Deep down inside, somehow I knew I'd never see Sean again. Oh Nick, I can't believe all of this is happening." She clung to him, so close.

"He's gone. It's a reality. I can't believe it. I'll never see his smile again, his laugh, his corny jokes, nothing." She pulled him closer. "I don't think he'll let us out of here alive. We know too much now."

"We're not dead yet. When the house is quiet I'm going downstairs to look around and see what I can do to stop that madman."

"Promise me you'll be careful?"

"Yeah I will. I'm not ready to die just yet."

She kissed him and held it, a long and lingering kiss, a surprise to both of them. "I've wanted to do that since I first met you. We may be dead by morning."

Nick wrapped his arms around her and kissed her. Then again.

He kissed her as if he had never kissed anyone before. They lay back on her bed, and she touched him, the touch of ecstasy. He had thought of this moment since he first met her. He could not stop touching her, kissing her, feeling her warmth and tenderness. *Katie.*

He wanted to hold her in his arms and never let her go, but she was not Katie. Katie was gone. April lay beside him but she was April not Katie and she wasn't Megan. *Megan? He suddenly missed her more than ever.*

She kissed him again.

He stopped her, "April… please," he said reluctantly moving her hand. "We need to talk," he said trying to catch his breath, the passion hoarse in his voice. "I think that it's a mistake for me to do this. I think that we need to talk and...," He stopped in midsentence and sat up in bed.

"What? What is it Nick?"

"Shhh."

Nick heard a distinctive muffled sound overhead—*whoomp, whoomp, whoomp, whoomp.*

"Get dressed. It's Blackhawks and they are right above the house. Let's go!"

"Blackhawks?"

"Blackhawk attack helicopters. The Marines are here." They rushed to get dressed and when they opened the door to leave he was standing there with a pistol in his hand. The gun was pointed right at them. It was Mevans.

Chapter Forty-Six

At eight A.M., the traffic was slow and sparse in the city of Potongang just on the outskirts of downtown Pyongyang, North Korea. Young men in drab military uniforms huddled in groups as they trudged past security inside the twelve-story building on Pulgun Street. The bike parking lot was already near capacity as the building filled with young military men all rushing to get inside.

After passing through the biometric scan, the men rode the superfast elevators to their respective floors. The tall non-descript building; built in 2012 had large windows facing to the outside but were covered in steel on the inside in order to deflect any attempt at eavesdropping.

Shai Nee made his way to his desk along with eighty other plebiscites or beginners. He smiled at his comrades as he sat down. Today was his day, the day he would strike a blow for freedom and the new dawn of Korea would begin. They had done this same procedure many times over the last three months and now he had been chosen to initiate the final data strike. When the handshake signal was received, a green light would appear on his command control console. He would raise his hand when it was lit and the signal would be given for the terrible data weapon to be activated. It was a supreme honor, and he was the chosen one.

Nee's hands began to sweat anticipating the glowing light being activated on his desk. He was afraid to look away, afraid he may miss something and his great honor would turn to a great disgrace. If that happened, his family would be banished to the farms in the countryside. He rubbed his hands together to keep them warm in the cold building. *Why won't it light? Why is it taking so long?* His tried to will it to turn on. *I command you to light. Give me the green light! Now!*

The green light flickered on, and he stood proudly to say, "Comrades, this is a day of victory for the great Republic of Korea. The green light is on. It is time!" He pressed the button. It was time.

His commanding officer stood, straightened his jacket, saluted him and breathed in a deep breath of satisfaction, "Today history is being made. Long live our glorious leader." He raised his hand to signal the technicians in the glass control room behind him to activate the data weapon. They were on a path to glory. "Death to all nonbelievers!" he commanded as he picked up the phone to call the great leader and inform him that the mission was underway.

The Digital Data Blast was immediately unleashed into the universe hurtling towards its target with devastating effect. The course was now set. People were about to die.

Chapter Forty-Seven

"Mevans?" Nick shouted in surprise.

The old man stood there looking at them before saying, "Follow me, sir. Quickly!" He handed Nick the gun, "You're going to need this. He's gone stark raving mad sir. It must be the uranium poisoning."

"Without a doubt," said April, always the physician. "Where are we going?" she asked as they walked down some old steel stairs, feeling their way against the wall, nearly in the dark. The walls were damp and the smell was musty. She heard the sound of running water.

"To the lab downstairs."

April stopped and said, "I'm not following you anywhere."

The old man turned to her and said, "I have something you will want to see. You must believe me."

They trusted the old man and followed him.

"Please hurry, there is not much time."

At the end of the stairs they pushed aside a heavy steel security door then down a long hallway and entered a glass room with steel animal cages stacked on top of one another on each side of the room. They housed snapping and snarling bloodthirsty hyenas on one side and lean hungry tigers on the other. The cross breeds, hyena from the nose to midsection with stripes around their haunches glared at them with their bright orange and blackeyes. The stench inside the room was horrendous. The floor was slippery under their feet.

April reached to one of the cages to maintain her balance on the slippery surface.

"Careful, don't get too close to them," Mevans warned. One snapped at her fingers inside the wire cage, nearly biting her. The room reeked of sulfur and the smell of rotting carcasses.

"These are the last of Dr. Schmidt's experiments. They are the crazy ones and they didn't turn out too well. Hurry! Please."

He opened a door at the end of the hallway and then turned the knob to a door inside a room off to the rear. A figure lay on a nearby bed.

"Sean!" she screamed.

Her brother managed a weak smile, "Sis? How the hell did you find me? Oh my God is it good to see you." She ran to him to help him, hugging her long lost brother.

Nick turned to Mevans, "Ahmed said he was dead and buried."

"I told you he was mad and sadistic. Why do you think he uses hyenas for guard dogs? Your brother was about to be killed by them when he was saved by Doctor Schmidt. It cost the good doctor his life. He saved your brother, and since then I have been caring for him as best I can. But he needs a doctor. Tell me what you need."

Nick grabbed the house servant by the arm, "Mevans, I must get to a computer and send a message to someone about the data blast. I need to get to Cole."

"Follow me, sir."

"April, will you be OK?"

"Yes, I'll be fine. Go, Nick. Be careful, he's a madman," she said kissing him as he left.

Nick grabbed Mevans arm and said, "Lead the way."

"Cole's room is up one level off of the garden."

"I need to get to him before the marines do. They'll shoot anything that moves."

The old man led him down another hallway and up some stairs. At the top step he suddenly tripped and fell, letting out a cry of pain. "It's broken, but go Mr. Ryan, hurry. His room is the second room off to the right."

Nick ran down the hallway and turned the knob, it was locked. He knocked but there was no answer, "Cole, it's me, Nick Ryan, open up." He heard some rustling in the room but the door stayed closed. "Open up, or I'll shoot the lock off." He pulled the pistol from his waistband and not waiting he pointed it at the door lock. He heard a click from inside and the door swung open.

"Boy, am I glad to see you," said the young techie.

"You have to help me."

"Nick, I thought all this was a game. That's what he told me, it was all going to be a game, a video game. But shit man, he's serious and he's crazy. This guy is nuts. He just left here ranting and raving."

"Yeah I know. I need access to a computer so I can send a message to Luke Garrison at NSA and have him stop the Data Blast. Now!"

"Sure, no problem, over here." The computer monitor lit up and Cole accessed the Internet. Nick typed in the information and sent it to Luke. His fingers tapped the keyboard anxiously awaiting a response and confirmation. It seemed like centuries and then finally it appeared on the screen,

DONE-
GOOD WORK-
LUKE.

"Now," said Nick pointing the pistol at Cole, "I need you to reverse your software commands and release control of the plane heading to Saudi Arabia and to Cushing and wherever else he's planning on bringing them down. And I need to have you do it now," he said cocking the pistol.

"I already started doing that right after he left," he said sitting back down at his computer. He tapped in the commands, then more, again and again.

"He's got a number of planes, including one coming in from Indonesia. I took care of the one going to Saudi Arabia first now I am doing the others. It will take a little while."

"We don't have a lot of time Cole. Hurry!"

He continued to furiously tap out instructions on the keyboard and then finally one last click. "Finished."

Spotlights circled the walls of the room and an unmistakable noise again filled the air, **whoomp, whoomp, whoomp, whoomp.**

"Follow me if you want to live."

"You bet. Right behind you."

Nick ran back to the lab with Cole right behind him. There was no sign of Mevans as they made their way back to the lab.

"God, who died in here?" asked Cole walking into the lab. "And what the hell are those things?" he looked at the deranged animals in the cages.

"Genetically altered hyenas. Stay away from them."

He smiled before he even saw her face but it quickly faded as he saw Ahmed holding her arm with the Glock pistol pressed into her side. Blood stained the front of his shirt. Mevans lay sprawled on the floor, dead.

"Drop the gun, Ryan. Do it! Now! Careful, I know how to use one of these," he said pointing the sinister looking Glock at his mid-section.

Nick dropped his gun.

"Well, well, my young protégée Cole. I'll deal with you later. For now, you will all be my shield to get out of here past the Marines and to my boat. Move."

"My brother is injured, he can't move," pleaded April.

Ahmed smiled a sinister grin. "I can fix that," he said pointing the gun at Sean's head.

"I'll help carry him," insisted Cole.

"Well, move it then. I don't have much time. Ryan you stay close to me and don't you even think about making a funny move. I'll shoot you dead, and you know I will. Move."

The caravan made its way slowly between the cages of hyenas all now fully alert, gnashing their teeth, hungry and looking for dinner. Their gnawed at the metal cages that held them back, their yellowing teeth tried to pull the cages apart. But even with their incredibly powerful jaws they were no match for the steel cages.

"Magnificent animals, are they not Agent Ryan?"

"Yeah, just not my favorite."

April reached for the heavy door and pulled it open. Ahmed and Nick waited as they made their way through the door with the injured Sean making a heroic effort to walk.

"Well Ryan, I knew you would come in handy for something. You will make a great hostage. They will never shoot one of their own." His bloody eyes glared at him. "Be careful, Mr. Ryan."

Nick froze, those words, he remembered those words from months earlier – from Del; *it was Koshari who spoke those words into his answering machine. It was Koshari who had killed his former partner. He had killed Del!*

He shoved Nick forward with the gun to his back and then the crazed lunatic turned to say goodbye to his animal charges. In that instant Nick pushed him backwards. The caged angry mongrels with the bright yellow and orange glaring eyes, angry eyes lunged at the cage door, demented tormentor. Koshari was caught off guard and moved back startled, losing his balance on the slippery floor, hitting his head on one of the cage doors. He was bleeding from the gash on his forehead. The door to the cage opened.

Nick quickly opened two more of the cage doors. The wild beasts bounded for the bloodied man, their tormentor lay on the floor as

Nick kicked the gun away and slammed the door shut. They heard bloodcurdling horrific screams as they left the room ... but then in a few moments it was all quiet. The catawampus were having their long overdue revenge. It was over.

April looked at him and said, "Thanks, Nick," she said still shaking from fear.

He smiled and said "Come on, let's go."

"Don't anybody move," came the command from behind them. It was the marines to the rescue.

Chapter Forty-Eight

The newspaper headlines told the world that an American president was finally able to bring together all competing clerics, religious factions and Middle Eastern Governments to discuss a ceasefire. They had agreed on a formula to live together in peace, at least temporarily, and found a way to stop the killing and bloodshed, which had racked the area for decades.

They were all to meet in Baghdad to sign the formal papers. There was still much work to be done but the groundwork had been laid and since the discussions began there had not been one suicide bombing attack in the region. Could it be the unthinkable, a lasting peace in the Middle-East? It was a fragile tenuous peace in a region not known for its quiet. But all they needed was one bombing and the bloodshed would begin anew.

Tuesday morning spectators lined the streets waiting for the emissaries of peace to meet in the great hall for the signing of the peace documents.

Mr. Tuesday walked among the crowds who were waving multicolored flags while singing and chanting religious hymns. It was a celebration the likes of which this part of the world has never witnessed. The bomb vest he wore was heavy, packed with pounds of explosives and filled with nuts, bolts, nails and ball bearings. The blood rushed to his brain, pounding his thoughts.

They would never sign this agreement he vowed to himself, peace was not good for a land that had only known bloodshed and terror. But people had grown tired of the old ways of death and destruction and honor killings. They wanted a place they could raise their children in peace. He would give them peace; he would blow them all to kingdom come… or to hell!

The cars with all of the dignitaries began to arrive at the grand meeting hall.

He walked in the shadows, counting the number of emissaries of peace including the new American president who had arrived. He made his way towards them. His path was blocked by crowds. *I need to get closer. I want to be in the center where I can see them die. All of them!*

He took a shortcut down an alley and walked through a small worn passageway and came up behind where they were assembled. He stepped back into the shadows so as not to catch the attention of the security forces that had assembled.

Passersby walked past him in the street without giving him a second glance, an old woman, a young boy and his flag and a big Chinese man.

Mr. Tuesday heard a noise behind that attracted his attention but it was too late. The silk garrote slipped silently over his head and wrapped around his throat. He could not breathe, he grabbed for the detonator now hanging by his side but he could not reach it.

The life was slowly being choked from him by the strong assassin. He fought with all of his strength, but the inevitable end finally came as he fell to the earthen floor beneath him. Chino pulled him into the cool darkness of the alley behind him and removed and disarmed the suicide vest tossing it aside in the trash.

Time to go home, his work was done.

Chapter Forty-Nine

The FBI liaison, Rich Reynolds briefed Nick on the operation as they waited for the plane to take them home.

"We were notified by the NSA as to your whereabouts after Director Jackson said he wanted to see you. We talked to Luke Garrison at the NSA and he told us what had happened, then we put all the pieces together. So we mobilized a task force to come and help stop Koshari's operation."

"What about the Data Blast from the Koreans? Were we in time to stop it?"

"Well, funny you should mention it but a North Korean fighter jet veered off course on a training mission, and as it happens he crash landed into one of their newest navy ships. Did a lot of damage to it and nearly sank it."

"And the Indonesian cargo plane?" Nick asked.

He chuckled, "There was a report of a huge explosion just off Christmas Island, with no transponder signal. But enough of this, time to go Mr. Ryan. I see your plane is here. Have a good flight home, sir."

The private government plane glided high above the Caribbean Sea winging its way towards South Florida and to home. April gazed out the window, lost in her quiet private thoughts. They both had words to say but neither wanted to speak. Her brother was resting comfortably in the front cabin compartment after being sedated.

Nick looked at her and smiled. *She looks so much like Katie, but there was only one Katie and that will never change. She's gone, and she'll never be coming back. It's time to let her go.* "April, can we talk?" he whispered.

"Yes…but let me go first," she said with that understanding smile of hers. He nodded his head. "Nick, over the time I have known you, I have found you to be kind, considerate, generous, caring and …, loving. Your wife was a very lucky woman to have you. But Nick, you need to understand, I'm not Katie."

"But April that's exactly what I wanted to talk to…"

"Nick, please let me finish. This is tough enough as it is." She stopped to gather her thoughts before plunging ahead.

"I've found the more time I spend with you the more I'm attracted to you and your quirky little ways. But I told you when we first met that I was separated from my husband. I travel so much, and he wanted more of me and of my time then I was willing or able to give him. I've decided to go back to him and give it another try. He's a good man…, like you."

"I understand," he said with a quiet resolve. "Since you looked so much like Katie I sometimes thought you were her and never really got around to getting to know you, the real April not the April I thought you were. And that's my fault because I think we could have been really good friends." His small smile made her laugh.

"Nick…we are good friends. Nothing will ever change that. We've been through a lot together and who knows someday I may be knocking on the door of your beach cottage again. I would love to have you meet Andy, my husband. You two are so much alike."

"I would like that."

The co-pilot came back inside their cabin, "You'll need to fasten your seatbelts we are coming into our approach to West Palm Beach International."

After they landed, they stood in the terminal facing each other in an awkward silence.

"You take care now Nick. You certainly made this an interesting adventure."

She leaned forward and kissed him, the sweet smell of her perfume lingering in the air as she turned and walked away to join her brother. She waved goodbye with her hand held high above her head without turning around. Soon she was lost in the airport crowd.

Nick waved, "Goodbye, April. Good luck."

The drive home was the quietest time he had alone in years. His thoughts and remembrances filled his mind pulling him in different directions. He needed to talk to someone. His father would have some ideas and his Uncle Nick… well he was Uncle Nick. As he pulled into his rocky driveway at the beach house, his life suddenly became clear. He knew what he was going to do. But first he had to pick up some beer and Jack Daniels for his dad and uncle. He knew it was going to be one hell of a birthday celebration.

Chapter Fifty

"Morning, Sheriff Carter. It's going to be another beautiful day in Vermont isn't it?

The smile was genuine as she looked to the blue Woodstock sky and replied, "Our little piece of paradise. Yep it's going to be another beautiful day Mrs. Mullen."

The tall sheriff continued her walk down Main Street and nodded to well-wishers who crowded the sidewalks on Saturday morning in downtown Woodstock. She paused at the front window of the Mountain Creamery ice cream store.

Some fresh pistachio ice cream would go down good right about now, she thought to herself. The small town chief of police gently pulled on her belt buckle in attempt to see how much room she had to spare.

"Go ahead Sherriff you can afford the calories. And I'll buy."

She spun around in the direction of the voice and saw him standing there with his broad shoulders, big boyish grin and that wild strand of hair dangling over his forehead.

"Nick! What the...? What are you doing here?"

"You said to come back when I knew what I wanted. I suddenly realized I knew exactly what I wanted and didn't want to wait a moment longer."

"Yeah, I know exactly what you mean," she said stepping closer to him, their bodies nearly touching. "Funny you should mention that but I've been thinking the same sort of thing."

"Great minds think alike."

"Then tell me what am I thinking?" she asked with that certain twinkle in her eye, her body pressing closer and tighter.

"Ice cream?"

"Close but..., no."

"Lunch?"

"No, but you're getting warmer. I never did get to show you my place on the mountain, did I?"

"No…, no you didn't."

She took his hand in hers and wrapped her arm around his as they walked down the street. Townsfolk smiled as they walked by down Main Street.

Reaching her patrol car on the side street parking lot, she called into her office. "Sherriff Carter to base. I'm taking the rest of the day off—over."

She looked at him and he pulled her close, her heart beating stronger than ever. They kissed the kiss of long lost lovers and she felt she was about to explode then added, "Base, I won't be in tomorrow either—over and out."

Megan draped her arms around his neck and kissed him. "I'm glad you came back Nicky, real glad. I missed your laugh, your touch but I really missed having you to talk to and be with, I missed that a lot. Life is good with you in my life. And it wasn't until just this moment that I realized that."

He kissed her hand, "You know Meg, just the thought of seeing you again kept me going so many times over the last couple of days. There is so much I want to tell you, to share with you. Hell, I don't even know where to begin. All I know is that I've missed you Meg, more then you could ever know."

"Let's go home," she said.

Nick got in his car and followed her through Woodstock and soon pulled into her driveway. When he looked at his cell phone he saw that he had ten missed messages. *Ten?* He started to check the unknown numbers when Meg grabbed his phone from his hands and said, "No more cell phones, not for at least two whole days. I'm not going to let this ruin our time together."

"You're right," he said, as they walked up the sidewalk to her house, arm and arm, together again, finally he was home.

-The End

Now, read an excerpt from where it all began:
The Potus Papers
A Nick Ryan Mystery Thriller

Chapter One

The Arabic message he texted was short and to the point. Yasim did not like texting about such sensitive matters, but time was of the essence. He had to let his father know quickly.

FATHER—
THE VIRUS IS LOOSE!
KITMAN MAY BE IN JEOPARDY.
URGENTLY NEED GLOBAL SPECIALISTS TO CONTAIN
AND INOCULATE.
THREE HAVE BEEN INFECTED BUT HAVE ALREADY
BEEN INOCULATED.
WILL PREPARE AN INOCULATION LIST.
WILL SANITIZE HERE.
I AWAIT YOUR RESPONSE.
YASIM

He looked down at the lifeless body lying at his feet in the center of the room. Blood pooled from the head, seeping into the rug.

Yasim searched the entire apartment again and once more found nothing. He was desperate. The more people who came in contact with what he was looking for, the more people would die. He did not care how many people died, but the damage it could do to the kingdom, to their world, and more importantly to his father's project, would be irreparable. It was imperative that he find it before it was too late.

He was going to need help, lots of help, but for now he had to keep searching. That was his job, the reason his father had dispatched him to Baltimore from the embassy in D.C..

The dead man, Joseph Santino, provided no clues. Yasim scoured the hallway before leaving apartment #802 and hurried passed #805, the former apartment of Hakim Maheed, a close friend of Joseph Santino. Yellow-and-black police tape still flapped from the wall across the apartment's entry door. Lifting the tape, he opened the door to Maheed's apartment for one last search. He had to find what he had been sent to retrieve or find some clues as to where it was. He had to, for he knew his father was depending on him.

• • •

The message received its predictable responses and caused some unanticipated consequences as it hit the airwaves on its way to Yasim's father, Prince Rashid, in Jeddah, Saudi Arabia.

"Jarim," Prince Rashid called out to his most trusted bodyguard, "get me a secure line. My son may wish to share this information with the Americans at the NSA, but I do not wish to give them any more than they may already have. I am sure they have this information already, thanks to my son. And if they have this information, I guarantee you the Israelis have it as well."

He shook his head in anguish. "How many times have I told my son not to use text to communicate such sensitive information as this? He tries to code information, thinking he will fool people. The Americans are not stupid—brash and vulgar, yes, but stupid, no. And this information of all things, the most sensitive information to our cause. What am I going to do with him?"

"He is young," responded Jarim. "He will learn our ways, I am sure of it." Jarim liked the prince's youngest son and always stood up for him whenever his father spoke ill of him.

"In battles you have only one chance to defeat your enemy, to be a man. If not, you perish. He has worked in our Washington embassy for too long. My son has been softened by Western ways and has grown accustomed to them, lax. I will need to handle it."

Jarim started to respond but the prince raised his hand to silence him. "I know, Jarim, you love him, as do I, but he must learn." The prince waved his hand for privacy and Jarim left the palatial suite.

Taking a deep breath, Rashid smelled the scent of the sweet desert flowers wafting through his high palace windows. The smell reminded him of his youth and the times he spent in the sands with his own father. He remembered the hunts, the raids, the battles, and the wild victory celebrations that followed. But today was no day to celebrate—today was a day to make decisions. The old prince coughed into his silk handkerchief and it turned crimson. He did not have much time. He had to act quickly.

He placed his phone calls and set his plan into motion. It must be stopped, and stopped now. They had come too far. They must not be defeated.

Chapter Two

Returning from lunch, Luke Garrison showed his National Security Agency badge to the first of three security guards at the NSA Fort Meade headquarters. They always surveyed his ID photo longer than anyone else's badge. The photo taken on his first day of work showed him with shorter hair and clean shaven, whereas he now sported long, curly locks of blond beachcomber hair and a full, reddish-black beard. He was a sight to behold for these security officials, who had no sense of humor.

After running his corned beef on rye sandwich, MP3 player, and backpack through the ultraviolet scanner, he was ready to return to his subterranean office to finish his work and hopefully get an early start on the weekend. Today he would like to get out of work at a decent hour see his fiancé, have some pizza and spend some time with her.

He pressed the elevator key thumbprint pad and inserted his badge into the security slot, then boarded the express elevator for a quick ride. The elevator traveled the thirteen floors underground in record time with hardly a vibration.

Jerry West was at his desk, poring over a pile of intercepts. "Did you bring me my ham 'n' swiss on rye?" he asked of his coworker. "Jesus, Luke, don't tell me you forgot again. You forgot my sandwich. Well, you are just going to have to sit here and cover for me while I run out and get my own lunch. Thanks a lot. I'll remember this the next time you want something from Epstein's Deli."

Luke had left his jacket on his chair because he did not need it outside on the unusually warm May afternoon in suburban Maryland. The cavernous computer room was another story. Luke swore he had seen it snow at times when the machines were running at top speed and the air conditioning rose to the challenge of keeping the computers cool.

Deep in the heart of the building, Luke wondered what he was doing. He had never anticipated that he would use his computer science degree from Caltech to sit in a huge computer warehouse just outside of Baltimore, poring over suspect telephone and text messages from around the globe.

Any moron could do this, he thought disgustedly. In his six years here, nothing exciting had ever happened, other than the time a mouse got into the computer room. The rodent drove everyone crazy, setting off the motion detectors until they caught it—luckily before it did any damage to the delicate equipment.

He leaned back in his chair, popped open his soda, and unwrapped his sandwich. He was alone in this cavernous room with only the multibillion-dollar pieces of hardware to keep him company.

What another day of drudge. He tasted the same old corned beef on rye that he'd been ordering since Christmas. After the Fourth of July, he would start ordering something different. Maybe he would go with ham 'n' swiss but skip the mayo. But he still had two months to think about it before making up his mind. Suddenly, the chatterbox display screen began to hum and the control panel lit up with all of the computers talking to each other in their rapid response format.

"What's going on?" he said to no one. He tossed his unfinished sandwich into the trash.

The machines increased their tempo. The red lights flashed on his control board. He spun his chair around and moved in front of his keyboard to take command. This is what he had been trained for, where the rubber met the road as they told him when he was hired. He was ready.

The machines continued at a fever pitch before beginning to collate and then assimilate the information and produce an intelligence report. This process used to take two to three weeks when he first came here six years ago, and now it was done in a matter of seconds. He retrieved the sheet from the high-speed printer and read the message:

Classified Agency Top Secret
Director's Eyes Only—Level Six
FATHER—
THE VIRUS IS LOOSE!
KITMAN MAY BE IN JEOPARDY.
URGENTLY NEED GLOBAL SPECIALISTS TO CONTAIN
AND INOCULATE.
THREE HAVE BEEN INFECTED BUT HAVE ALREADY
BEEN INOCULATED.
WILL PREPARE AN INOCUALTION LIST.

WILL SANITIZE HERE.
I AWAIT YOUR RESPONSE.
YASIM

Process Immediately according to Protocol Level Six.

Message sent from CONUS (Continental United States) to KOSA (Kingdom of Saudi Arabia)— Unscrambled message from Crown Prince Yasim in suburban Maryland to his father, Saudi Prince Rashid, Jeddah, Saudi Arabia. Of note, origination point is same building as residence of the late Hakim Maheed.

Message transcribed from Yasim at 13:52 Zulu time — via Motorola text phone model #2034A, nonsecured communications tool. —End

Wow, what a hot potato! *Luke wished he had gotten Jerry his sandwich because he could really use his help now. After a few moments' deliberation, he finally picked up his phone and followed protocol, calling the Intelligence Director, Jack Drury, a Staff Naval Commander.*

"Commander Drury, please. Analyst Garrison calling with a Level Six message." This was the highest level message Luke had ever seen. He had level twos before but never a level six. Protocol required that all level six communiqués have an immediate response at the highest levels, rather than in the Blue Book that was collected at the end of the day.

"Bring that to me now," was the immediate response when Drury's aide, Colonel Parker Johnston, picked up the phone. "Mark it 'Level Six, ROTC—Reporting of Terrorist Communications—Director's Eyes Only.' Bring it to me STAT."

Luke grabbed his tie off the coat rack in the corner of his office and sprinted toward the elevator, tying his tie in the process. After three attempts, he finally completed the complicated procedure, just as the door opened on the executive floor of the building. He was greeted at the elevator by Colonel Parker Johnston. Luke shook the big man's hand in silence and they started their long walk down the green carpeted hallway.

Drury and Johnston had been in the CIA together during the wild days of intelligence gathering before being removed from the field and assigned desk jobs at NSA headquarters. They had crossed the line using unauthorized interrogation techniques on prisoners to gather information to save the life of one of their field operatives who'd been kidnapped. They got the information one hour too late and their associate was found dead two days later, beheaded.

Drury and Johnston were still in the doghouse with the bureaucrats because of the way they got the information. Now they were both looking for something that would redeem them and get them back in the field.

Johnston reviewed the contents of the intercept as he and Luke Garrison walked. When he finished reading, he stopped walking and turned to Garrison, asking, "Has anyone else seen this?"

"No, sir, no one." Luke straightened his crooked tie.

"Keep it that way. Don't mention it to anyone. Do you understand? No one."

"Yes, sir."

"Okay. You are free to return to your office, but remember, do not tell anyone of this document. Am I clear?"

"Yes, sir, perfectly clear."

Colonel Johnston turned and left the young computer scientist to find his way back down the long hallway and prepared to discuss the Intercept Report with his boss, Jack Drury.

He closed Drury's door behind him, not really wanting to interrupt his long-time friend today of all days. Today was the beginning of Drury's annual hearings in front of the closed Congressional Committee on Intelligence Funding. Never a good day for Jack Drury.

But Johnston had to bring him up to date. He handed him the report and waited. Drury nodded then they talked for over fifteen minutes until NSA Director Drury finally asked his trusted aide, "PJ, what's your take on all of this?"

Johnston leaned back in the worn brown leather sofa and studied his friend. "The same as you, Jack. It's not what it appears to be. Somebody has an overactive imagination, but I detect the same undercurrent as you and I don't like it one bit. We need to send this to the CIA and FBI, now."

"What about...?"

"Yeah, get your coat, we're going for a little ride to the White House. The president needs to see this. I'll have Mary call over and tell them we're on our way."

He pressed the intercom button and immediately his loyal assistant came on the line. "Yes, sir?"

"Mary, please contact the White House and tell them I need five minutes with the president."

"Yes, sir."

He grabbed his coat and called down for a car. He was on his way to see POTUS—the president of the United States—Cerab Hussein.

Chapter Three

Clarisse Dubois stepped out of the taxi, her short cocktail dress riding high up on her thigh, and paid the leering driver. She liked to walk the last couple of blocks toward her apartment in the Montparnasse section of Paris, especially now, this early May morning, when the air was filled with the scent of jasmine and roses. Her apartment was on a one-way side street and it added extra to the taxi fare to go around the block to drop her directly in front of her building.

It was brisk when the sun went down, but she loved this time of year. She was happy that at four A.M. her day was finally over. The previous evening, as many times before, she had been in the company of boring rich men, but last night was worse than she ever remembered. She was used to them standing taller and leering down her dress, trying to catch a glimpse of her cleavage and well-shaped young breasts.

Clarisse was not familiar with the Arab custom of constantly talking business in Egyptian, Sudanese, Farsi language, or whatever else they were speaking. Continuing to smile, she had waited for them to finish so she could leave and go home.

Not too bad, she thought, reviewing the evening in her mind. *At least they had great food.* The evening had been worth it. She had made some good money just smiling and laughing with these old men—not on her back, which was fine with her.

So distracted in thought, she did not notice the man who had followed her from the corner where the taxi dropped her.

She missed her Hakim and was excited to talk with him earlier in the week after he arrived back in Washington, D.C. on his way home to Baltimore. She only had to wait another three weeks before he would return to Paris. Perhaps they could then picnic again in the park by the Seine. She so enjoyed a picnic on the slow river that ran through Paris, lying underneath the tall dragging branches of the willow trees on the isle in the middle of the scenic river.

A shuffling noise sounded behind her, interrupted her idyllic thoughts. She walked a little faster and shot a glance over her shoulder, checking, while she fumbled for the tear gas spray in her purse. A man in a dark business suit, tall and slight, with hair the color of night walked rather intently behind her, carrying a suitcase, but he did not seem to be paying much attention to her.

He crossed to the other side of the street and she made her way inside her iron gate, running up the steps of her apartment building. The outside of her building was full of deep shadows. The streetlight was flickering off and on in front of her building and she made a mental note to call the building manager the next day to have it fixed.

She pulled the house keys from the outside pocket of her purse and was soon safe inside. Once there, Clarisse breathed a sigh of relief. She had remembered that some of the other girls had encountered many overeager clients, who would follow them home to offer them more money for massages or extended pleasures.

Clarisse was tired and only wanted to soak in the tub; it had been a very long day. She sat at her desk and pulled out the business cards she'd accumulated over the last two days and decided to file them tomorrow. *Never know when you may need a contact or two.*

She checked for messages. No message from Hakim on either her machine or her cell phone, but then she remembered the time difference. He was probably still in bed—hopefully alone, she chuckled to herself. She unbuttoned her sheer silk blouse in the hallway while making her way toward the kitchen refrigerator to pour some wine before her bath. Tomorrow she would sleep in. What a relief.

She did not bother turning on other lights, for she knew the layout of the apartment by heart. The light from the moon and the flickering streetlight, which shone its whitish-yellow light through her front windows, allowed her to navigate her way.

Her apartment was large and rather lavish by Parisian standards, with four tall front windows, and ornate wall panels lining the hallway to the one large bedroom. Hakim fell in love with it the first day he saw it and signed the papers for her on the spot. It had become his home away from home when he was not in the States or traveling in the Mideast.

She missed him more than she cared to admit.

The young part-time model perused the contents of the fridge and was pleased to see she still had some red wine left over from a previous evening. She poured a large glass and re-corked the vintage wine bottle, shoving it into the rear of the fridge, and then grabbed the last orange off the shelf.

She did not see or hear him until she closed the refrigerator door. It was the man who had followed her to her building. She gasped and dropped her wine and orange at the sight of him and both crashed to the floor. Before she could scream, the knife was quickly at her throat and his hand gripped the hair at the back of her head.

"My money is in my purse, there on the chair in the foyer. Take it all! Just leave me alone, please." She wanted to cry but she was afraid that was just what he wanted. She held her tears and her fear in check. He raised the knife, glistening from the soft light of the moon outside coming through the side window and pointed it at her, motioning her toward the bedroom.

She did not recognize him from tonight's affair or any other, for that matter. She thought hard, trying to remember if she had seen him somewhere but no luck. Her pace quickened as she looked for a place to run and hide. The bathroom, maybe, but it was at the other end of the hall, behind her.

His silence was unusual. They all seemed to want to talk, but he was different. Her fear grew as they walked quietly through her apartment. She could yell, but that would only enrage him.

Clarisse led the way into the bedroom, the one place she felt in control, even though he had the knife and still held her by her hair. He watched her every move. She recognized the long knife as one from her kitchen.

When they reached the bed, she turned to face him, her blouse totally unbuttoned and her breasts swaying in the soft light of the room. They did not seem to catch his attention. At age twenty-nine, sexy, pretty, and well built, she was in the flower of her youth. She had men pretty well figured out—she knew what he wanted.

He pointed toward the bed, now dangling four yellow silk ropes from the serrated knife blade. He motioned for her to lie down. Now she knew exactly what he wanted. He wanted control. She knew his type. Most times they would tie you up, sit in a chair, and be pleasured by the mere fact of having a woman lying helpless before them. She caressed the bright cutting edge with her finger as she pulled the yellow silk ties from his weapon. She knew the drill.

She tied both of her ankles to the posts at the foot of the bed, then she tied one of her wrists to the headboard. The other wrist she left untied, waiting for him to complete his fantasy. She faked a moan, trying to get this over with as quickly as possible, so he would leave and she could finish her warm bath and pour another glass of wine. He tied the last rope then put duct tape over her mouth. It was only then she noticed he wore light green surgical gloves.

He came close and sat next to her on the bed, stroking her hair, parting her blouse with the knife tip, admiring her anatomy. A red crescent star tattoo graced his right wrist at the base. She had seen many of those tattoos this evening on the bodyguards of the guests, but she dared not ask its meaning.

She searched his eyes and was terrified to see, staring back at her, eyes containing no emotion or passion. His eyes were black, like a shark's before an attack. Fear rose in her throat again as she approached unknown territory. He was not like the others.

His hand slid down her stomach and parted her legs, slowly cutting off her lace panties before he laid the knife on the bedside table. She tensed her body and he moved closer to her, reached under her head as if to kiss her. She lay there beneath him, helpless, but acting like she wanted him, when in reality she wanted it all to be over. She had difficulty breathing only through her nose. Her breaths were coming quicker, shallower.

He was still fully dressed when he removed a pillow from beneath her head and leaned closer, so close she knew he could smell the Chanel perfume she'd dabbed between her breasts. She raised her hips slightly from the bed, waiting, resigned to her fate. Smiling, totally in control, he took the pillow from beneath her head and suddenly pressed it over her face, pushing down hard. She shook her body to the left then to the right, trying to get free. She tried to scream but her voice was muffled. She tried to call out for help but the screams were trapped by the heavy tape. She tried to get free. She needed air, fresh air, heavenly air.

She twisted and squirmed fiercely to be rid of the pillow that was drawing the life from her body. She couldn't breathe. His strong arms held the pillow firmly in place. Her nose and mouth were covered, she'd lost all control, and she panicked as she realized what was happening. She was bound tight with the silk strands by her own hand. How stupid she was!

She was gasping for air but found none. She tried to take a breath through her nose but no matter how she tried she could not get away from the smothering pillow. She was too young to die! Her last thoughts were of Hakim and how she missed him. Her body went limp.

Jasara left the pillow on her lifeless body. His pulse never rose; he was calm as if sitting, reading. He surveyed the room, seeking any telltale signs of his presence or clues that he'd ever been there. When he found none, he walked toward the front door of the apartment, peeling the abandoned orange that was no longer needed by its former owner. When police found the body, they would think the obvious, a sex play gone wrong. Not an execution, or as his employer liked to call it …, an inoculation.

He strolled past the just-opening crêperies, raising their shutters to release the sweet smell of crepes into the air. The street cleaners hummed their relentless task of keeping the Paris roadways clean.

The tall, thin man hailed a taxi at Rue de Rennes and headed for the airport, just as a light rain began to sprinkle the streets.

He headed to the airport. He'd been busy the last couple of days, flying in from Istanbul the day before, Cairo the day before that, and Indonesia before that, where it all started. He was on his way to Washington, D.C. and the next name on his list. He knew that time was money as he hurried to his next rendezvous. He unfolded the heavy blue paper containing his list while the taxi made quick headway to Charles de Gaulle Airport in the early morning traffic. The next name on the list was Palmer, Richard Palmer in Baltimore.

He was next on the list to die.

Chapter Four

The Season, as the locals called it, was over in Palm Beach County. All the wealthy snowbirds and socialites had flown on to their next nesting destinations up north and out west. You could now get a parking spot anywhere you chose, have dinner without making a reservation, and encounter no lines at the supermarket. The weather in early May was faultless—every day warm and sunny, a Chamber of Commerce kind of perfect.

Nick Ryan stirred from his bed, hearing the coffee maker utter its final gasping wheeze as it squeezed the last drop of moisture from the reservoir. Steam and the strong smell of Brazilian coffee wandered through his oceanfront apartment.

The breeze coming off the ocean and the smell of salt air stirred through the open crack in the sliding glass doors in his apartment above Caffé Luna Rosa. The slight wind caused the sheer curtains to part.

His apartment was on the top floor over the restaurant, and if you did not mind the sound of people talking and laughing at ten-thirty at night, it was the ideal penthouse apartment. It was right across the street from the beach at the end of bustling Atlantic Avenue, right on Beach Route A1A, in the quaint little town of Delray Beach. The apartment next to his was occupied, but he had not met the other tenant, even though Nick had been there for over a month.

Caffé Luna Rosa was one of many busy and hip restaurants on A1A facing the beach, but it was the only one with rental apartments above them. Nick's father was the one who remembered seeing the rental sign during dinner one evening. Nick was staying at his father's beach bungalow, but had been forced to vacate it after a rogue wave flooded out the fifty-year-old surfside cottage. The contractors seemed to take forever to finish the reconstruction job, aided in part by the Palm Beach County building inspectors. They were not crazy about a house that close to the ocean, and while they could not deny a permit, they did everything in their power to slow down the process.

For over a month, Nick's father had been recuperating from surgery on his back to remove an old bullet fragment that had moved dangerously close to his spine. Now he was in a special rehab facility in Boynton Beach, fifteen minutes away.

Nick rolled over in bed and was greeted by a smiling picture of Katie, his wonderful, but now deceased, wife. He looked at the photo longingly and said good morning. She did not return the hello. God, did he still love her, and oh, how he missed her. He could hear her calling him to join her. Whoever said grief got easier with time was dead wrong.

Katie's picture was placed strategically on the table at his bedside next to a scrap of paper containing the only haunting clue to her brutal murder. It was a yellow sheet of paper with the names Jessie and Linda handwritten, plus a series of numbers starting with 561, the area code for South Florida. The phone number belonged to no one. The other digits were a mystery too. Jessie and Linda were ghosts, nowhere to be found.

Other numbers were scattered on the small scrap of yellow paper. He could not find their names in Katie's cell phone, home phone, office, Rolodex, computer, Blackberry, nothing. He had even searched through her desk at her office in Baltimore at the Theoretical Applied Physics Lab, or TAPL, as the employees called it. No luck. Nick continued to search for other clues for over a year. He was at a dead end, finished. Nothing.

He opened the drawer to the bedside table to begin his daily ritual. Nick reached inside and pulled out the black-and-silver police special. He wrapped his fingers around the cool, indifferent pistol, a Smith & Wesson .45 caliber, with only one bullet loaded in the chamber. He spun the cylinder around like a wheel of fortune, and after kissing the picture of his beloved Katie, he placed the revolver to his forehead and pulled the trigger. A loud click echoed throughout the apartment. He was spared to live another day.

His thinking was distracted by the sound of a female voice coming from just outside his apartment, through his sliding patio door, speaking what sounded like fluent Italian. He threw on an old pair of lifeguard beach trunks over his boxers, slid on a t-shirt, and grabbed his coffee. The traffic noise was picking up outside and he checked the time on his alarm clock. The cracked glass panel read eight-fifteen A.M.

Nick pushed aside the sheer drape that sailed in the breeze and stepped outside to the cool, sunny morning, another glorious day in paradise. The sound of the voice grew louder as he approached the end of the balcony. On the porch next door, sitting in a chair, was a woman with a pair of gorgeous, athletic legs. She wore a tight-fitting expensive silk jacket like Katie used to favor. She had shoulder-length auburn hair, with huge, gorgeous curls caressing her neck, but her back was to him and he could not see her face. *Lord, let her face match the rest of her*, he said to himself, as he leaned on the railing overlooking the street below, cradling his old FBI coffee mug between his hands.

She was still talking on the phone when she stood up and turned around, gesticulating with her hands. Yeah, she had to be Italian. Then she noticed him. Slightly startled, she looked directly at Nick, then smiled. She finally blew a kiss into the phone and said, "*Nonna addio*, bye, Grandma," before turning her attention to Nick.

"Good morning, neighbor." She grinned and held up her phone. "My grandmother is from the old country and doesn't speak English too well. I try to help but what can you do?"

Nick grinned in response.

She picked up her coffee mug and walked toward him and along the divider that separated the two balconies. "I'm Rose, Rose Scalese. But everyone calls me Rosa." She smiled while cautiously surveying him up and down. She liked what she saw.

"Nick, Nick Ryan," he replied. The cars below them had stopped, blasting their horns, probably waiting to stake their claim for a prized beachfront parking spot.

"I haven't seen you before this," she said. She was tall and her high heels made her appear that much taller. She must have been a model at some point, for her facial features were soft and her clothes were ideally tailored and color-coordinated. Her figure matched her attire perfectly from everything he could see.

"I've been doing some traveling up and down the East Coast," he stammered as she unbuttoned her fitted jacket, revealing both a Glock pistol on her hip along with a police ID dangling from her neck. But his attention was soon diverted. He was right; she was built like a model.

"Let me officially welcome you to the neighborhood," she said, as she saw him eyeing her badge and weapon. "I'm with the DEA, Southern District. I hear you work at the Bureau."

Nick did not immediately respond. He did not like to talk about his work at the FBI. He'd worked there over five years before taking a leave of absence last year after his beloved Katie was murdered.

"I was, but I am officially on a temporary leave of absence now."

Since he joined the FBI, he had lost his mother, his older brother, his wife, and now he looked after his father as he recovered from surgery. He did not blame the Bureau for his troubles, but he also did not believe in coincidences.

"Join me for dinner tonight? My treat?" Rosa asked, changing the subject.

"Sure. Where and when?"

"How about meeting at City Oyster Restaurant on Atlantic Avenue, down on restaurant row? Seven?"

"Sounds great," he told her. "You don't want to do the café downstairs?"

"No. Not tonight. I would love some fresh fish."

"City Oyster it is, then."

She turned to leave, but, thinking better of it, stopped and faced Nick. "Oh, Nick, no offense, it's not a fancy place, but you will have to shower and shave. Some fresh clothes without coffee stains would also go a long way for us getting a decent table." She smiled, her eyes twinkling with humor. "By the way, I'm named after the Rosa in Caffé Luna Rosa. My parents were good friends with the owners. See ya tonight, Nick."

"Rosa, don't worry. They tell me I clean up pretty good. See you tonight," he said with a chuckle.

She walked away but turned halfway around to get another look at him. She waved before disappearing.

Nick hummed the haunting melody, "The Hills of Yesterday," the theme to the movie *The Molly Maguires*, which he'd watched the night before, while he headed down the back stairs, across the street, and out onto the beach for his morning jog. It was time to check on how the reconstruction was going with his father's beach bungalow. He was looking forward to it being finished and moving back in with his dad. It was the closest thing to feeling like home. Technically, home was Baltimore, but that was a long way from here both geographically and emotionally. After Katie died, he closed up their house in Baltimore and left for Florida. He had not been back since.

His usual jog down the beach was accompanied by the surf pounding on the shore and the splash of salt spray in his face. He was frequently joined by other early morning joggers, but today there was no one, and his thoughts wandered. Maybe his life could change. Maybe it wasn't too late. He missed his Katie. God, did he miss her.

He finished his jog. Time to shower. He stripped off his clothes, but once again, his thoughts were hijacked by Jessie and Linda. *Who the hell were they?* And what did they have to do with Katie's death? He would find out, regardless of how long it took him. The Smith & Wesson .45 lured him to the side table with its cold, come-hither smile. The steel weapon felt warm in his hand. He felt lucky today…

~

16677892R00110

Made in the USA
San Bernardino, CA
13 November 2014